A HORSE
FOR ALL
SEASONS
COLLECTED STORIES

A HORSE
FOR ALL
SEASONS

COLLECTED STORIES

BY
SHEILA KELLY WELCH

A YEARLING BOOK

With love to my husband, Eric,
and
In memory of Tony, Dublin, Flash, and Stubbs

Published by
Bantam Doubleday Dell Books for Young Readers
a division of
Bantam Doubleday Dell Publishing Group, Inc.
1540 Broadway
New York, New York 10036

"Worthless Penny" and "Frosted Fire" first appeared in the May
1989 and January 1994 issues of *Cricket* magazine.

ISBN: 0-440-41174-2

Reprinted by arrangement with Boyds Mills Press, Inc.

Printed in the United States of America

December 1996

10 9 8 7 6 5 4 3 2 1

CWO

CONTENTS

A HORSE FOR ALL SEASONS

– SPRING –

THE LONG MARCH

March had come in like a lion but was refusing to go out like a lamb. For days a cold, relentless rain had been pounding the barn, saturating the ancient wood.

The mare moved restlessly along the perimeter of her roomy box stall. She dropped her nose and sniffed the hay she'd been given early in the evening. It held no interest for her now. Her attention was being drawn inward, to the foal she'd been carrying for eleven months.

Across from the stall, the young Border collie stirred in his nest of straw. The mare's movements had disturbed his sleep, pulling him from his dream of a wide, sunny field dotted with obedient sheep. He lifted his pointed muzzle and sniffed the air. One of his black ears poked up while the other rose only halfway, giving him a lopsided, quizzical expression. Those ears could tell him a lot. Right now he knew that the mare had moved to the back of her stall near the door.

Rosey had given birth before, but her other foals had come later in the year, when the weather was kind. Now she shoved against the stall door, searching for warmth and soft grass.

A week before, the door's metal latch had broken, and since then the boy, Josh, had been propping an old wooden fence post against the outside as a brace. He didn't want to bother his dad about getting the latch fixed. Caring for the mare was Josh's responsibility—his horse, his job.

It hadn't been his father's idea to buy the mare at the farm auction. Sheep, that's what he'd had in mind for himself, and for Josh, too. But that warm fall day Josh had looked at nothing except the scrawny roan mare tied in the narrow stall. The auctioneer had seemed almost apologetic as the mare was led out, blinking in the unforgiving sunshine.

Most of the farmers had turned away and directed their attention toward the farm machinery that lined the driveway leading to the farmhouse. Josh was one of only three people who had bid on her.

Rosey hadn't cost much. Not long after they'd brought her home, Josh realized he'd gotten more than he'd bargained for, although he liked to put it another way: A bargain. Two for the price of one.

Lately Josh had been worrying constantly about Rosey and the foal she was expecting.

"Relax," his father told him. "Nature'll take care of things." Josh was not reassured.

The night was nearly half over when the rain gave up. Just outside the stall door was a large puddle circled by slick mud. As Rosey pushed her nose against the wood once more, the brace began to slip. Her nostrils dilated at the scent of fresh, cool air that contained a tantalizing hint of spring. She pressed with determination. The door swung outward slowly and stopped, leaving a three-foot opening. Rosey plowed through, oblivious to the pain as her broad sides scraped along edges of door and doorjamb.

For a moment her restless discomfort was forgotten. She lifted her head and let the wind ruffle her mane; then she started across the barnyard. With each step her hooves sank deep in the muck. She had gone only a few yards when an angry gust of wind slammed into her eyes. The stall door banged shut. Its brace slipped into a lower position, firmly planted against the door.

Rosey dropped her head and swiveled her body to present her tail to the wind. She snorted at the cold, soaked ground. No, this was not right.

When the door thumped shut, Kip hopped up and followed his ears and nose across to Rosey's stall. He sniffed the emptiness and whined anxiously. But he didn't bark. He seldom did. His job was to work with the sheep, and a yapping dog was not much help. Kip was a silent, intense partner when Josh's father needed to move the sheep.

The horse was not any of his business. When she'd first arrived, he'd tried to herd her. Rosey had given him a few sniffs and one halfhearted kick. Gradually they had become companions, if not friends.

Now Kip missed her presence inside the barn. He liked order and routine but had no way to deal with this minor disruption. He returned to his bed and found that one of the cats had taken over the warm spot. Nosing her over a few inches, Kip curled up beside her with a sigh.

The wind was picking up. Rosey, made anxious by the turn of events, stared at the door. She felt an urgent need to get to a safe place, and now the stall was blocked off. Usually the door was propped open during the day to allow her free access to shelter. Only at night had Josh been confining her to the stall.

For several chilly, damp minutes she stood grimly by the door, waiting. The only movement came from within her body.

Abruptly Rosey's head came up. She pricked her ears and turned in the direction of the pasture and the woods beyond, where a hill and trees promised shelter from the wind. She moved in a slow but steady walk, slogging her way through the mud and out the open gate into the pasture.

At first she kept to the trail leading down the gradual slope toward the creek. When she entered the woods, she had to swerve and pick her way among the trees and underbrush.

Rosey came to a jutting boulder. Her way was barred by a fallen tree that formed a natural fence, and she had neither energy nor desire to struggle through the lattice of trunk, branches, and twigs.

She stared dully at the small open space beside the rock. After pawing the leafy ground, she lay down and let her body take over.

The foal was a filly, dark and wet, with a broad blaze and large, limpid eyes. Rosey scrambled up. One front leg banged against the trunk of the fallen tree, but she felt no pain. She had work to do.

Soon the tiny filly had been licked clean and was nearly dry. She was on her feet, unsteady but strong, and she began to nuzzle along Rosey's flank. Her moist nose bumped gently against her mother's body. She was searching, vaguely at first and then with increasing purpose. Finally she found the warm, sweet milk. Her tail flicked back and forth in excitement as she savored the first meal of her life.

Rosey heaved a sigh of contentment despite the wind and an occasional spatter of rain. But she was tired. Normally she would have stayed on her feet, protecting her new foal, but she was not a young mare, and the strain was beginning to wear on her. When the filly stopped nursing, Rosey gave her one more lick and then settled close to the fallen tree.

Kip was awakened for the second time that night by the scrabble of a cat's claws. The fur on his neck rose of its own accord, and as he stood up he heard the desperate squeak of a rat. Kip dropped back onto his haunches and scratched behind his tipped-over ear.

Shaking the loose strands of straw from his glossy black-and-white coat, he trotted to the ragged opening in the side of the barn that served as a door for him and the five resident cats.

He hesitated. Turning his head, he sniffed quickly and located the cats, some sleeping and some hunting, and the young sheep dozing in the far stall. He smelled fresh hay and sodden wood walls. The empty horse stall still bothered him. He scrambled through the opening and out into the muddy barnyard.

A blast of wet wind hit his side, parting his fur and running a shiver down his back legs. For a moment he stood undecided. Then he turned to the left and began his customary check of the farm and its inhabitants. The sheep came first, for they were his job. He found them huddled safe in their shelter, unharmed by the short blasts of wind that skipped over the hills and around the farm buildings.

The creek was next. Lately Kip had found it exciting. Changed with the rains, it had swollen over its banks and was filled with new odors. He splashed along in the water, moving with the current until he reached the woods. There the scents of tiny creatures lured him from the creek. He leaped out and shook his sodden fur. Then he snuffled through the weeds, his tail waving frantically in anticipation. He pounced and missed. As he raised his head, another smell reached him.

Kip dashed through the underbrush toward the pair of horses. A few yards away he stopped and froze. The moon appeared from behind scurrying clouds. Its pale light was reflected in Kip's gleaming eyes.

Rosey snorted and thrust her front hooves in front of her body, the first step in getting up. But because she'd lain so close to the fallen tree, both forelegs slid beneath a tough branch. She struggled but was unable to rise or withdraw her legs. Simply and effectively, she was trapped.

Kip eyed the two animals. He knew Rosey quite well, but the foal smelled strange. New and yet familiar. Puzzling.

One thing was certain to Kip: These animals belonged at the barn. His job was to watch over the farm animals, to move them when necessary. Kip approached the mare cautiously, remembering being kicked. He thumped his nose against her rump, but all she did was swing her head in his direction. Next he grabbed her tail with his teeth and pulled, bracing his forepaws on the moist earth. There was no way his forty-five pounds could budge her nine hundred.

The long-legged filly watched, her nostrils quivering. Uncertain fears crowded her mind as she sidled closer to her mother.

Realizing that the mare would not move, Kip focused his attention on the foal. He needed no human to instruct him. His herding ability was innate. He moved between the filly and Rosey, glancing back and forth. He was a determined black wedge driving between them.

The filly resisted. Her mother was her source of shelter, food, and protection. When she finally turned away, confused, Kip took advantage. He leaped behind her and forced her to step forward. Then, using the obstacles of brush and branches to aid him, he drove her slowly along through the dripping woods.

The terrified filly stopped frequently and tried to turn. But the black blur was always ready for her, nipping and shoving, back and forth.

When they reached the trail, Kip's spirits lifted. Here was the track to the barn. Here the sheep always went quickly, hurrying toward home. But Rosey was home to the filly. On the trail there was more room, and she whirled and headed back.

Kip bounded in front of her and turned her again. He was low to the ground, his tail down, eyes burning. Now he was more vigilant, as close as her shadow. The woods ended and the pasture stretched before them. In a lightening sky, the clouds chased across the moon. The filly hesitated as wind nipped her tender nose.

She tried to turn, but the dog defied her, blocking her path. She ventured out into the open a few steps, and Kip moved up, attempting to drive her forward. This maneuver left the trail unguarded, and the foal whipped back.

Kip dove in front of her and felt the glancing blow of her tiny forehooves. Rolling over, he came up running, but the filly was already well ahead of him. She would have plunged on to the creek if Rosey hadn't whinnied.

Kip skimmed over the brush, trying to cut her off. But she was quick and wild with fear. Each time he managed to get in front of her, she simply ran over him.

In a few moments she was reunited with her frightened dam. Rosey struggled again, thrashing, but the branch was unyielding.

The filly rubbed her nose against Rosey's back in greeting and nickered softly. Rosey let her head drop. All the fight had left both animals.

Kip, panting, sank to the ground and eyed the horses. Guarding the mare and foal was better than nothing, yet he still felt compelled to move them.

His frustration mounted, and he whined anxiously, then barked once. The sound was startling. He barked again, with more force, then rose to a sitting position and let his head fall back. With his nose pointed skyward, he howled a long, thin wail of despair.

Josh rolled over and tugged the blankets tightly around his chilly back. He burrowed deeper into his pillow, blocking out the whine of the wind. Then, like a drowsy turtle, he blinked and peered out his window. The sky showed a hint of dawn.

Often in the past week Josh had gotten up early and gone out to check on Rosey. Now he shrugged off sleep with his blankets and stumbled onto the cold floor. As he pulled on jeans and stuffed his toes into heavy boots, he kept his teeth firmly clenched to prevent chattering.

When Josh reached the barn and turned on the

light, he noticed two things. There was no bouncing Kip to greet him, and no sleepy-eyed Rosey peering out of her stall.

Josh crossed the open space and stared blankly.

But I shut the door last night, he told himself. His mind refused to accept that Rosey was gone even while his chest tightened with fear.

Grabbing a flashlight off its shelf, Josh retraced his steps. Outside he circled the end of the barn and directed the beam of light slowly across the barnyard.

Nothing.

He glanced once at the dark house. Waking his parents would waste time, and the mare was his responsibility. Besides, he thought, she might be just behind the end of the barn.

He didn't want to think about the thirty acres of murky woodland and an old mare who could be in trouble. Maybe she'd slipped into the creek. Or she could be sick or hurt and unable to nurse a newborn foal. Josh sucked in his breath, knowing that every second counted.

Slipping in the mud, he entered the pasture.

And where's Kip? he wondered as his light revealed nothing.

"Here boy! Kip, come!" Josh's words were buffeted by the wind and tossed away.

"Rosey!" Josh tried to whistle, but his chilled lips rebelled. Stooping low, he examined the wet earth. Hoofprints! He got up and followed them along the trail toward the woods. The flashlight beam bounced and tripped over the terrain before him, beckoning him forward. As he entered the woods, he noticed that the hoofprints looked muddled, confused. He breathed shallowly as he continued walking. He swept the light across the dense wall of trees and brush. How could he ever find her? A sharp bark stopped Josh in his tracks.

"Kip! Where are you?" One more excited yelp answered his question.

Josh headed in the direction of the sound. He crashed and staggered through the woods until he reached the tiny clearing next to the boulder. His light caught Rosey's nervous eyes.

"That'll do, Kip."

Licking and squirming with delight, the dog leaped against Josh's legs.

Josh knelt beside the mare. A sick feeling gathered in his stomach. Out of the corner of his eye he was aware of the tiny filly lurching to her feet. But his main concern was with Rosey.

"Take it easy, baby. What's the matter?" he crooned, patting her neck with trembling fingers. As if to explain, the mare made another attempt to rise.

"Whoa. Easy. Don't try. You're stuck, but I'll get you out." Anxiety gnawed at the pit of his stomach. Had Rosie already damaged her legs in the struggle?

Josh climbed over the tree branch and tried to pry it up, but it would not budge.

The filly nosed her way around her mother, looking for the sweet milk she'd enjoyed before.

Josh glanced at her, bit his lip, and said, "I have to go back. Kip, stay!" He took off at a run.

The dog sank to a crouch position, his eyes fixed on the filly. He waited silently, intent on his job.

Sunrise began to streak the eastern sky with the colors of peaches and tangerines. By the time Josh returned, clutching a saw, he was breathing hard.

He stroked the mare's neck, soothing her and himself. Then he carefully examined the branch that held her prisoner.

"Steady, girl," he whispered, shoving a rock beneath the branch to serve as a brace. He began to saw.

Rosey was too exhausted to distrust him. She stared and twitched her ears.

When the branch was almost severed, Josh paused. His hands ached and sweat dampened the hair across his forehead. He checked to make sure the rock would prevent the branch from falling on Rosey's legs. Then he finished sawing, grabbed the offending limb, and swiveled it away.

Kip rose with an expectant look, but the mare lay still.

"Come on, girl," Josh pleaded as he picked up the saw.

Rosey swung her head and looked at her foal.

With his hand clenched tightly on the saw handle, Josh waited.

Finally the mare planted her forelegs and lurched up with a grunt. She nuzzled her foal and nickered.

Josh ran his hands down her legs but found nothing worse than scraped skin. He waved at the rising sun and cried, "We did it!"

Kip bounded over for a pat on the head. Then he moved to one side, eyeing boy, mare, and filly as they started on their way toward the barn. He trotted behind, herding them joyfully into the bright new day.

HAND-ME-DOWN HORSE

"Guess what!" I shrieked at my mom as I made a mad dash across our muddy lawn and leaped onto the porch. She stopped sweeping.

"Aren't your feet dirty, Carrie?"

"Mom, no! I jumped over all the sloppy spots. Didn't you see me?" Honestly, my mother acts as if I'm about six years old. I guess it all comes from me being the youngest of seven kids. "See?" I practically stuck my foot under her nose, hopping around like an idiot.

"Fine, dear," Mom said. She went right back to chasing a sprinkling of spring blossoms off the painted wood. Now, personally, I like flowers on the porch, but Mom has this warped view about things she considers dirt. I was about to give her my opinion when I remembered.

"Guess what!" I said, not waiting for her to answer. "They're here!"

"Who?" Mom asked as she glanced anxiously at the long driveway between our farmhouse and barn. Mom has this thing about unexpected company. Basically, she panics. I think it's a leftover from when all seven of us kids lived at home and our house was always messy enough to be condemned by the health department. Now, with just Rob and me left, our place is spotless. . . well, almost.

"Not *here*," I told her, shaking my head. "At Carlsons' old place. The new people moved in yesterday."

"That's nice. I hated to see that lovely house empty."

Actually, I think Mom was still wishing we could've moved into Carlsons' place after they retired to Florida. It doesn't look like a farm—not like our place, anyway. It's got this gorgeous stone house with a landscaped lawn, a perfect horse stable, and even a riding ring. My dad laughed when Mom sort of hinted that maybe we should sell our farm and move over there.

"You know what the real estate people call a place like that?" he asked. "A farmette. Can't you just see us living there with our seven kids, forty cows, a horse, two dogs, eleven cats . . ."

"Don't forget the calves," Rob reminded him.

"Dad, didn't you know that Marmalade had five kittens?" I asked.

"We really only have two children left at home," Mom said.

"Don't rejoice, dear," Dad said. "Soon summer

vacation will arrive, and the three in college will come home to roost."

"They'd better not roost," Rob said. "I need some real help with the haying." He looked at me. The trouble is, I'm sort of small for my age, and most of those stupid bales weigh more than me.

Anyhow, that was about as close as my mom got to living on a fancy farmette.

Meanwhile, back on the porch, I was just about to tell Mom that these new people looked like they were perfect for a farmette when the screen door banged, and my darling brother came stomping out.

"Aren't you going to ask him if his feet are dirty, Mom? After all, he just came out of his bedroom, and the yard is lots cleaner than that."

"Now, Carrie," Mom said.

"I need the car," said Rob.

"He needs it to take Melissa Ferguson for an ice-cream cone. He told Jason that'll soften her up and she'll say yes to going to the spring dance with him. I mean, he'd have to buy me six banana splits before I'd . . ." I quit talking to hide behind Mom.

"You'd better stop listening to my phone conversations!" Rob yelled.

Now why can't he have a sense of humor like me? I mean, that's my one good trait.

"Guess what!" I said real loud, hoping to distract both Mom and Rob.

"You've decided to move out?" Rob asked sarcastically.

I gave him my most withering look and said, "We have new neighbors. And they've got horses!"

"We've got one, too, unless old Splashes turned into a cow last night." The sad thing is, Rob thinks he's funny.

I leaned back against the porch railing. "These are show horses. Black Arabians, like the Black Stallion. There's a girl named Stephanie Reynalds, and she was riding around that neat riding ring they've got, training Mystery. That's the horse. And she's got one of those hats, and fancy boots, and everything."

"A horse with a hat? Sounds just right for a farmette," Rob said.

"You can't have the car," said Mom as if the rest of our conversation hadn't happened. "Dad's taken it to town. You'll have to take the truck."

"The truck! Aw, Mom . . ."

"There's nothing wrong with it." Mom was sweeping the porch steps now.

"Yeah," I chimed in. "Melissa will be so charmed by your adorable smile, she won't notice the mud, straw, dents . . ."

Rob slammed back into the house, probably to call Melissa.

"Be sure to smile into the phone!" I called after him.

"What did our new neighbors have to say?" asked Mom.

I shrugged. Actually, I'd done most of the talking. "Well, I asked that girl Stephanie if she'd like to go riding with me and Splashes up on Raspberry Hill. We'd only have to go along the highway partway. But she says her horse is only for shows. Mystery might get hurt or scratched."

"That's too bad," said Mom. "I'm sure you'd love to have some company on trail rides."

Mom doesn't like me to go alone 'cause she worries I'll fall off and break my head or something.

"Yeah," I said. "But I wish even more I had a horse like Mystery. I mean, Splashes is okay. He's great on trails, but he's almost twenty years old, and he isn't really mine."

"Of course he's yours, Carrie. You know Rob gave him to you last summer."

"Right. When Rob got his driver's license, I got an old Appaloosa. He's just a hand-me-down horse!"

Mom came back up the steps and took one more halfhearted swipe at the porch; then she turned and looked at me in this funny way she has.

"What's the matter? I got a milk mustache or something?"

Shaking her head, Mom came over and took my chin in her hand and tipped my head this way and that.

"What?" I blurted.

"Just as I thought. There's a tinge of green spreading all over your face."

"Aw, Mom. Don't start with that green-with-envy stuff again. Please! You've been telling me that for years."

"But, Carrie." Mom gave this exaggerated sigh. "Some days I feel as if I'm living with a little green alien."

I guess Mom has a point, but I wasn't about to admit to her that I was jealous of Stephanie Reynalds and her fancy show horses. I have a reputation for being envious of all the other kids in our family. After all, for as long as I can remember, they've all been bigger than me. And I've always wished I had long fingernails like my sister Marnie, wavy auburn hair like Susan, blue-green eyes like my brother Michael, long lashes like Sean, a pretty singing voice like Lisa, and even Rob's cute smile (not the smirk he saves for me, the nice one he uses for girls like Melissa Ferguson).

Anyhow, that night in bed I decided to stop being jealous of all my sisters and brothers and concentrate on Stephanie. As I listened to a thunderstorm grumbling and complaining off beyond Raspberry Hill, I began to imagine myself riding Mystery in a horse show. Stephanie had come down with mono or something awesome like that, and she'd asked—no, begged—me to ride for her. Naturally, Mystery won first prize. I could almost see that big blue ribbon.

A gigantic crash of thunder brought me back to my bed. I guess the storm wanted to let everybody know it'd finally climbed over Raspberry Hill. I sighed and rolled over. I would just have to face it. There was no way ol' Splashes would ever win me a ribbon—blue or any other color. It didn't matter how smart he was about loud cars and yapping dogs—he'd never make a show horse. I began to count the raindrops splatting against my window. Pretty soon I was picturing little green aliens tapping to get in. Then I must have gone to sleep.

The next day was Saturday, and we were all eating breakfast together. Rob was giving Dad his best grin and saying "You won't need the car this afternoon, will you?" when somebody began pounding on our door.

My mom jumped up and jammed all the cereal boxes back into the cupboard, and our two dogs started barking. When Rob got up to answer the door, my cat Paula jumped on the table and began licking Rob's toast. Mom grabbed her and put her in the laundry room.

"Who is it?" Dad yelled.

"Some kid about a horse," said Rob.

Leaping up, I almost knocked over my chair. Maybe Stephanie was starting to feel sick and wanted me to practice for a horse show.

When I got to the door, she was standing there with a halter in one hand. Her pretty face was all scrunched up, and her long blond hair hadn't been combed. She sure looked sick!

"Our horses!" she sort of spluttered. "A tree fell during the storm. It knocked down the fence, and they both got out. My dad's looking for them. He's afraid they'll get hit on the highway. I . . . I forgot to shut them in their stalls last night."

At that moment I didn't feel one bit jealous of Stephanie. "I bet they crossed over into Kerns' alfalfa field," I said. "You go look, and I'll get Splashes."

Even though my horse is old, he's still plenty fast. I figured I could do a lot more looking on him than I could do on foot.

I ran to the barn, jerked the bridle off its peg, and charged out to the pasture. I guess Splashes was too startled to protest, because he let me slip the bit right into his mouth. I hooked the throat latch and tossed the reins over his head. Now came the hard part. Just in case Stephanie was still hanging around watching, I was not about to lead him over to my favorite tree stump. Instead I took a deep breath and jumped up and over his back. Splashes started to prance. There I was, only half on. But I pumped with my legs and managed to scramble up.

We trotted briskly out the gate toward the highway.

I squinted into the morning sun. In the field across the road, I could see the two Arabians putting on a show. They were galloping across the short growth of alfalfa with their tails and noses in the air. They swerved away from Mr. Reynalds, who was shouting and shaking a pail of oats. Wild with freedom and the rain-fresh air, they swept toward me and Splashes. Their hooves pounded the tractor trail that emptied onto the highway.

The Arabians couldn't see the two huge trucks that were lumbering up the hill and rounding the curve. The drivers of the trucks couldn't see the horses either. I could see everything from my side of the road, and my heart felt like it jumped right into my throat as I hoarsely screamed "Stop!"

Splashes saw the horses, too, and gave an impatient tug on the reins with his head. I don't remember deciding—I just loosened the reins and leaned forward.

With a bound, Splashes took off. I'd never, ever galloped him across the highway. Not this time, either—we flew! Splashes knew the trucks were bearing down on us. He must have. Maybe he enjoyed racing against death. I didn't look as that first truck raced toward us. The driver laid on the horn and almost split my ears, but I held on tight and let Splashes do it all.

We made it!

The truck passed behind us with a slam of air and sound that knocked us head-on into the path of the galloping Arabians. They twirled and reared and said hello with excited nickers. I pulled Splashes back into a walk. He arched his neck and let out a little squeal.

Stephanie ran over to us. "Thanks, Carrie!" she exclaimed as she slid the halter over Mystery's head. "I didn't even see those trucks. If you hadn't gotten across and stopped my horse, she would have run right in front of that second one for sure."

Next Mr. Reynalds came huffing over, his smile almost as wide as his scarlet, sweaty face. But his first words sounded like my mom's: "Don't you ever pull such a dangerous stunt again, young lady. You're lucky you didn't get yourself and your horse killed!"

I shrugged. Luck had nothing to do with it, I thought. Splashes knew he could beat that truck, or he wouldn't have tried it. He's that kind of horse.

Mr. Reynalds added, "But it was great! A real blue-ribbon performance. Can't thank you enough."

"Thanks . . . I mean, you're welcome." I felt kind of foolish and happy, too.

When we got back home, I said to Splashes, "You know, I have bitten-off fingernails, scraggly brown hair, gray eyes, short lashes, I sing off-key, and I've got a crooked smile. But from now on, I don't care. You know why?"

I leaned over and gave his thick neck a hug. Then, after I spat out a few strands of mane, I told him, "Because I've got you! A hand-me-down, blue-ribbon-performing horse!"

For once Splashes answered. He snorted! But I ignored him.

WORTHLESS PENNY

"Richie! Richard Brian Johnson!"

I sat up in my rumpled bed, suddenly awake. When Mom yells my full name, I'm in trouble.

I blinked at my clock. No, I hadn't overslept. It was Saturday, and earlier than I usually get up to help Dad with farm chores.

"Richard! That pony of yours got into the garden. Dad's furious. Hurry!"

I scrambled out of bed, tripped over my own feet, and crashed onto the floor. The kids at school don't call me Bigfoot for nothing.

"Richard? What are you doing?"

"I'm coming, Mom!" I jammed my bare feet into the first pair of shoes I found in the jumble under my bed. Not bothering with jeans, I ran downstairs and outside in my pajamas. I took one deep, shaky breath of the spring air, then charged toward the garden.

There they were. Dad's face was purplish-red from chasing Penny, and a useless rope dangled from one hand. Across the garden stood Penny. She had one ear cocked toward Dad while she yanked tops off the young corn plants.

"Hide your rope!" I called. "Let me get her."

Dad gave me one of his think-you're-smart-don't-you looks and put the rope behind his back.

"Hi, Penny," I said in a soothing voice as I stepped over the rows of corn. The dew-laden leaves brushed against my legs and soaked through my thin pajamas. Just yesterday I'd hoed and weeded this sweet corn. Penny chomped into another plant, jerking it out of the ground. I sighed.

Worthless, that's Dad's description of Penny. In a way it was true. I hadn't been able to ride her for over a year. It isn't just my feet that are big; I'm the tallest kid in my class. Already people ask "How's the weather up there?" When I sit on Penny, my toes brush the grass. Since I'm the only kid in my family, there's nobody to ride her.

As I walked carefully toward her, I knew what Dad was thinking. He'd said it before: "I'm a farmer. Don't have time or money for useless pets."

Penny pricked her ears toward me and snorted.

"Okay, girl. See? Maybe I've got some oats." I held my cupped hand toward her, and the old glutton couldn't resist sticking out her nose for a whiff.

Taking one giant step, I wrapped my arms around

her neck. She gave a sigh and stood still. Dad grumbled over to us and shoved the rope into my hands. While I fashioned a makeshift halter, he said gruffly, "Put her in the barn. She must've found a break in the fence, or made one. Next week I'm putting a Pony for Sale ad in the paper. You fix the fence, Richard, after chores."

"Sure, sure," I muttered as Dad stomped away. Do this, Richard. Do that, Richard. What did he want from me? Did he really expect me to sell my pony?

Penny nudged me affectionately, and I rubbed her copper-colored neck.

"Okay, I forgive you." To prove I meant it, I put her in the stall and gave her some oats. I used to feed her special treats every day and ride her all over the farm. Now that I'm older, I've got to help Dad. There's a ton of work on a farm, and thanks to Penny I had to add fence-fixing to the load.

"But don't worry," I told her. "We're friends. I'm not going to sell a friend."

The rest of the weekend I spent my few spare minutes with Penny, feeding her apples and trying to think of some way to convince Dad of her worth.

I even tried tying her in the backyard to let her trim the overgrown grass. When Dad noticed, he bellowed, "Get that animal off the lawn before she poops!"

I went to Mom for advice. She just gave me a big lecture about Dad having to work so hard to make a living at farming. "It isn't easy for him either," she said. "Can't you at least try to understand his point of view?

After all, Richie, you hardly pay attention to Penny anymore. Don't you think she'd be happier in a new home?"

"No! She's happy right here!" Nobody understood how I felt, and nobody cared.

I didn't get my big idea until Monday, and it came to me at school, of all places.

Our class was working on plans for the annual school carnival, which was less than a week away. Our committee was still arguing about what to do for a booth.

We were in the hallway watching Andrea, our chairperson, tap her pencil impatiently. "Come on, where are the ideas you promised to think up over the weekend? Everybody else is practically finished."

John waved his hand frantically. "I know! We'll have a spitting contest! No, better yet, a dunk-the-principal booth."

Andrea rolled her eyes.

"I have it!" John said. "We'll have a freak show. Richie can be the Tall Man, and he won't even need stilts."

"You guys!" Andrea shrieked when I poked John's arm. "Stop it. *I* have a real idea. We'll have a fortune-teller's booth."

"That's dumb," said John. "We'd need costumes and junk like that. It's a worthless idea."

Andrea began to sputter.

Worthless? "Hey, how about a pony ride?" I asked.

So that was my big idea for saving Penny. It wasn't great, but I thought Dad would have to admit that she was being useful.

That night I asked him if he could drive Penny to town for the carnival. He nodded and kept reading the paper.

"Dad?"

"What, Richie? I told you I'd do it."

I shrugged. "Just wanted you to know that the kids on my committee are excited about having a pony for our booth." That was only a slight exaggeration.

"Fine. But there isn't a carnival every week."

I wouldn't give up. "Penny doesn't eat much. Can't we afford to keep her?"

Dad laid down his paper and gave me a steady look. "That's not the point. You must know how I feel about anything or anyone with a lack of purpose. I won't have a useless animal on my farm. The ad starts tomorrow in the paper. You know, son, the money from that pony will be yours. You could buy yourself a nice new bike or whatever."

"I don't need a bike! You just don't care about Penny or me!" I ran up to my room and slammed the door. The rest of the week I kept myself shut away from my father. Even when we were together, I hardly talked to him. Mom looked worried, and Dad acted more tired than angry.

The stupid ad ran in the paper, and we got some calls. One woman decided Penny would be too small for her children. A little girl said Penny sounded perfect, but she planned to keep the pony in her basement.

Saturday the sun shone hot and bright on our

carnival. John pretended Penny was a wild bronco, which scared some kids and disappointed others. Andrea whined about the heat. Penny pranced and munched and enjoyed all the petting. I guess our booth was at least as good as the slingshot game, where half the tiny kids shot their own tummies.

By the end of the day I was tired, and Dad was late picking me up. There were just a few parents, teachers, and kids left cleaning the playground when a lady came over to me. She had a wide, friendly face with freckles and wrinkles.

"I'm Janet Whitten," she told me. "I'm in charge of the handicapped riding program over at Shady Acres Farm."

I nodded, not knowing what to say. I'd heard of Shady Acres, a big horse farm about an hour from our place. And I'd read an article about the handicapped riding program. All I could remember was the newspaper picture of a grinning kid on a fat pony.

"I'm looking for several more ponies to buy, and I was impressed when I saw your mare. She's so patient and sweet-tempered, even on a sticky day with lots of kids. Any chance you'd sell her?"

"No." I shook my head hard and fast.

Penny shoved at my hand, asking for another treat. She had enjoyed the day, with all the love and attention, but it was time to take her home. Dad would never know this lady wanted to buy her.

"Well, if you change your mind, just call Shady Acres. We'd love to have her."

As Ms. Whitten turned to leave, I saw the picture of

the happy kid in my mind. That pony could be Penny. Maybe I suddenly understood Dad's point, or maybe I just realized I didn't have to sell a friend to share one.

"Wait!" The word jumped from my mouth. "Penny's not for sale, but"—I hesitated—"you could borrow her for as long as you'd like." Ms. Whitten smiled, and I grinned back as I added, "She's a very valuable Penny."

A Horse for all Seasons

– SUMMER –

MULBERRY MAGIC

The car was hot. Brenda rolled the window all the way down and leaned her head out as far as her seat belt would allow. Next to her sat her youngest brother, Cody, with his chubby bare leg sticking to her thigh. But she couldn't move over at all because on the other side of Cody, jammed together, were Jamie and Michael.

"We need a van," Brenda told her parents.

"Right," said her dad. "But we need a bigger home more."

Brenda sighed as best she could in her squished condition. Shopping for a new van would be more fun than driving around every weekend searching for a larger place to live. She imagined herself in an air-conditioned car showroom, running one finger daintily along the sleek side of a luxury van. It would be snowy white with fuzzy blue seats. "We'll take this one," she'd say, as if buying a car were as easy as picking out a ripe orange. She'd climb inside and take a deep breath, savoring the unique scent of a new car's interior.

"I gotta go potty," said Cody.

Brenda glared at him, and she was suddenly aware of the odor of sweaty little boys. In her daydream there had not been any Cody. Or Jamie or Michael either.

Their mother turned around, her flushed face framed in dark curls.

"How bad?" she asked.

Cody, sucking his thumb, didn't say anything. He shrugged, his hot little arm sliding up next to Brenda's and then down again.

"Just hang on," said their mother. "We're almost there. I'm sure the real estate man will let you use the bathroom in the house."

Brenda stared out the window, distancing herself from her family, getting ready to transport herself somewhere else in her mind. For a moment she hesitated, caught within the confines of the stuffy car, wishing that she had a magic wand so that she really could change her life, not just pretend.

It wasn't that she hated her brothers. It was simply that she felt outnumbered, and their apartment had no space. That's why this place they were going to look at today might be interesting. It was a house. In the country. With five acres of land.

Shutting her eyes, Brenda saw a huge white house

with soaring pillars and a willow tree gracing its marble stairs with lovely sweeping branches. Tara, she thought, just like in *Gone With the Wind*.

Cody began to jiggle up and down on the seat next to her, jolting Brenda back to reality. We'd better get there soon, she thought. The ultimate embarrassment would be meeting the realtor with a little brother in soggy pants.

"This must be it," said her father, but his tone was not as sure as his words.

"Really? Oh," her mother said flatly.

Brenda's eyes popped open. No, it wasn't Tara. The car was bouncing over a rutted driveway. Cody moaned plaintively. They were approaching a mottled gray house that looked as if it might have once been white. It made Brenda think of an overgrown, slightly scorched marshmallow that had been squared off and plopped onto the flat prairie. There were no pillars. There was no willow tree. Parked in the driveway in front of a sagging wire gate was a battered pickup truck of uncertain color.

"Is that the real estate guy?" asked Michael doubtfully. A husky man in coveralls was lounging against the front of the truck and smoking a cigar. They were accustomed to realtors who looked as if they'd just stepped out of a TV ad for toothpaste.

"Maybe this isn't it," said their mother.

But the man leaned over and tipped his cap as if he'd been expecting them when they neared his pickup, so they stopped.

"You the Felkers?" he asked. "Good. Don't have much time. Mr. Smythe got called off on some big deal, and he asked me to show you around."

As Brenda and her brothers piled out of the back seat, their parents introduced themselves to Mr. Jennings. He wasn't a realtor, but the owner of the house, and he lived "down the road a piece" himself, he told them. The last set of renters, young people, had up and left without much notice, so now he was interested in getting a nice family settled in.

They all went through the open gate, except Jamie, who walked around it. There was no fence—just a gate suspended between two listing metal posts. Mr. Jennings mumbled something about "fixin' the fence" as he led them up a sidewalk made of large uneven stones.

The inside of the house was dingy, with the smell of old food or mold in every room. But Brenda realized that her parents were pleased with the size of the house, the rent that Mr. Jennings mentioned, and the fact that the toilet worked.

Brenda didn't form an opinion about the place until they all filed out the rear door. There was the backyard, with a tire swing hanging from a tree branch. A dilapidated garage and a shed with a broken window were huddled together off to one side. Beyond a ragged barbed-wire fence was a bunch of trees that could almost qualify as a woods. And just on the other side of that fence, nibbling on not-quite-ripe mulberries that dangled from a low-hanging twig, was a white horse.

"Oh," said Brenda.

"A horse!" cried Cody, hopping up and down.

"Yeah, sorry about that horse. It's sort of a problem," said Mr. Jennings. "Those young people, the ones who were here last, bought him. But they couldn't take him when they moved. Tried to tell me he was partial payment for the rent they still owed me. I got nowhere else to keep him. Plan to sell him at the livestock auction next month—not that he's worth much. I hope you won't mind looking after him for a while."

"We don't know anything about horses," said Brenda's mother hesitantly.

"Mom! I do," Brenda said, surprising herself with her exclamation. She continued with determination, "I've read everything. And I've got my own book about horse care that Grandma gave me for my birthday. I'll take care of him. Promise! Until Mr. Jennings sells him."

So it happened. The Felkers moved to the country. Brenda had space, even her own room, and a horse, as if by magic, she thought. So she named him Magic.

She took some of her hard-earned baby-sitting money to buy brushes and a hoof pick at the hardware store in town. As she set the items on the counter, she felt a thrill of ownership. This stuff is all for *my* horse, she wanted to say, even though that wasn't exactly true.

Magic seemed to enjoy his grooming sessions, especially since Brenda was always certain to give him a piece of carrot or an apple whenever she brought out the brushes.

In the shed she found a dusty old blanket, a saddle, a

halter, and a bridle. Magic was patient about letting her fiddle with buckles and straps while she learned how to put everything on him properly.

Riding was the big step. Brenda had only been on ponies a few times, and Magic's back looked forbiddingly high. She enlisted Michael's help in holding the horse's head while she pulled herself up into the saddle. The first ride was just back and forth on the driveway. But within a few days, Brenda and Magic were venturing out onto the gravel road. From then on they went out daily, usually in the late afternoon or early evening, when the day's heat was seeping away into the surrounding fields and birds were flying lazily and calling softly to each other.

They would amble along, Brenda daydreaming and Magic dropping his head to snatch a mouthful of grass every so often. Cars passed them in puffs of yellow dust. Sometimes Brenda waved, but often she was too involved in her fantasy world to really notice anyone.

Each day was a new adventure. One time Magic was an old racehorse whom she'd stolen from cruel owners. They were escaping to Blue Valley, where she would set him free to roam unfettered for the remainder of his days. She would find a cave and live there in the wild with Magic forever.

Another day Magic was a unicorn and she was a fair maiden. They were on their way to a magic kingdom where they would meet a wizard who'd tell them how to free the earth from a dreadful drought. As she rode, Brenda scanned the clear expanse of sky, looking for clouds. There were none. She urged Magic into a trot. They must hurry before the earth dried up and cracked apart, releasing the monsters who lived beneath its surface. Brenda shivered despite the warmth of the low-slung sun on her shoulders.

Sometimes she pretended that she was a Native American girl named Raven who was riding her horse across the prairie. She had gotten separated from her family when they were attacked by settlers, and now she was crisscrossing the land, searching for her parents and her three little brothers. But she couldn't find them, even though sometimes she saw pony tracks in the dirt, and once she had come upon the dead, smudgy ashes of an abandoned campfire. Seeking a sign, she raised her head and gazed out over the prairie. A smoke signal? A soaring eagle pointing the direction? But there was nothing, just the land rolling away like a great buffalo hide that had been shaken wide and smooth.

"Isn't it boring walking around on that horse day after day, week after week?" asked Jamie.

"No."

"He's not really yours," said Michael. "You shouldn't act like he is."

"Shut up."

"I wanna ride," said Cody. "Please?"

"Okay." So Brenda helped Cody get up on the saddle in front of her, and they rode along the powdery road.

"You know something?" she asked Cody. He shrugged, his thumb in his mouth.

"I think pretend is better than real, don't you?"

Cody nodded, and his hair brushed against her chin, tickling slightly.

"Okay, see, pretend you're my little boy. My son. And your name is Jeremiah."

Cody nodded again.

Inside her head, Brenda continued the story. Jeremiah's father—her handsome husband—had been badly injured by a bear that had invaded their small homestead near the foot of the mountains. She had driven off the bear by banging her largest and heaviest pot with a metal spoon. Now she was riding to town to fetch the doctor. They must hurry. Their horse began to trot, but Jeremiah bounced so hard he yelled, in Cody's voice, "Ow! Help!" They had to slow to a fast walk.

When they got back to their yard, Michael said, "I told you so."

"What?" asked Brenda.

"I told you he wasn't your horse. Mr. Jennings called. He's coming tomorrow to take Magic to the auction and sell him."

"Off, Cody," Brenda said, lifting him down.

She unsaddled Magic, and as she worked her eyes felt singed. The air seemed unnaturally dry, scratching her throat with each breath, making it feel raw and tight. But she didn't cry, even as she hugged Magic's warm neck and kissed his soft nose.

All that long June night Brenda struggled to think of a way for her and Magic to escape. But each of her plans would work only in a fantasy world. This was real; she had no magic wand to save him. Tomorrow Magic would be gone.

A vision of the auction crept into her mind. She could see her horse being led out into a ring, surrounded by staring people. "I'm looking for a younger horse," one man said. "I don't think he's very pretty— not what I had in mind," grumbled a beautiful girl with braces on her teeth. "I don't think he looks strong enough to carry me," said a very big boy.

What if no one wanted to buy him? For a moment Brenda dared to hope. Maybe Mr. Jennings would bring him back. "Too bad. No buyers," he'd say. "I guess you'll just have to keep the old nag." But then a sickening thought occurred to Brenda. Horses could be used for meat as well as for riding. What if the only person interested in Magic was a meat buyer? Brenda's heart pounded like a crazed windup toy.

Somehow she had to make Magic look good, too good to be sold for meat.

Early the next morning, Brenda dragged a moldy, stiff hose from the basement and hooked it to the outside spigot. She had decided to give Magic a bath to make him sparkle so he'd dazzle the eyes of the buyers at the auction. Then someone special would buy him, someone who'd love him the way she did.

She went into the pasture and caught Magic, led him out into the yard, and tied him to the tire-swing tree. As she dragged the hose over to him, he eyed it apprehensively.

"Don't worry. It's just water," she told him. "Like a summer shower." But Magic danced away from the gentle spray and kept moving and fidgeting until Brenda's face was pink with frustration.

"You need help?" asked Michael sympathetically.

Brenda nodded.

Michael stood on the other side of the horse and leaned against him so that Brenda could hose him thoroughly.

"Hey, you're getting me wet!" Michael yelled.

"Me, too!" cried Cody, racing to the scene of excitement and shoving his dark head under the droplets.

The water quit abruptly, and when Brenda looked back along the hose, there was Jamie, holding it in a kink and laughing.

"Thought I'd do the ol' horse a favor," he said. "I can see he likes showers 'bout as much as I do."

Brenda waved the hose nozzle threateningly at her brother, and he dropped the hose to dive for cover behind the tree trunk.

Finally Magic's coat was wet through, and Brenda used an old scrub brush and a touch of shampoo to lather up his back and sides. He relaxed and nibbled at some mulberries that had dropped from the tree. They were ripe now, juicy and large.

"Wow, look at all that dirt," said Jamie, obviously impressed at the filthy gray rivulets that ran down the horse's sides.

"I'm getting out all the old dirt that the brushes

couldn't reach," said Brenda. "And besides, he hasn't had a bath in years, probably."

"Lucky!"

The boys hung around while Brenda rinsed off Magic with the hose. But when she started combing his tangled mane and tail, they wandered off. She missed their wisecracks; they had taken her mind off her reason for bathing Magic. She pressed her face against his wet neck and blinked away tears. "I'll miss you," she whispered as she set to work finishing his forelock.

"Sissy!" Cody came clumping down the back porch steps. "Mr. Jennings! He's inside talkin' to Mommy."

Not already! Brenda untied Magic and put him back into his pasture. She gave him a good-bye kiss on the nose and then raced toward the house, hoping to slip in the back door and go hide in her bedroom.

"Whoa, there, missy!" Mr. Jennings's booming voice caught her as he came around the side of the house. "So you're the little horsewoman. Just talked to your mom. Glad to hear you've been taking great care of my horse."

Brenda nodded and swallowed. She didn't know how to get away from the man without seeming rude, so she scuffed along next to him as he headed toward the pasture.

"Hey! What's going on here?" asked Mr. Jennings. "That's not my horse!"

Brenda blinked. A beautiful horse was standing at the gate. His soft brown eyes were identical to Magic's, but instead of a shiny white coat, this horse had a white coat with purplish-black spots.

"My horse is definitely white. This one here is a horse of a different color." Mr. Jennings's voice sounded quite serious. Cody stared intently through the gate at the splotched horse.

With a dramatic shrug of his shoulders, Mr. Jennings added, "I can't very well sell the wrong horse, can I?"

Brenda looked up at the hulking man. His face was lined and brown, but his eyes were like specks of bright summer sky. "And, of course," Mr. Jennings continued, "I can't sell a dirty horse either." He paused. "How would you kids like to take care of this horse for me?" asked Mr. Jennings.

"No problem!" Brenda said. Then she asked hesitantly, "For how long?"

Mr. Jennings peered at the horse, chuckled, and said, "For as long as you like."

After thanking Mr. Jennings and watching him drive away, Brenda climbed onto the gate. The dark-spotted horse reached out and sniffed her knees. She smiled. "Hey, that tickles! You just go away and roll some more. Don't know why I ever bothered to give you a bath." She leaned forward and straightened his sparkling white forelock. "Mulberry magic," she whispered.

"What, sissy?" Cody mumbled around his thumb.

"Let's go riding," said Brenda. "I'll be me. You can be you. And Magic can be . . . a magician."

Cody took his thumb out of his mouth with a pop and said, "Yeah!"

COSTUME CLASS

The colt had no intention of leaving the security of his mother's shadow. He was usually curious and enjoyed exploring every corner of his home pasture, but the noise and activity of his first horse show were overwhelming.

He pricked his ears at the sputtering loudspeaker. He snorted at a hat that was lifted off a young contestant's head by a gust of wind and came wobbling and bouncing across the show ring. He pawed the ground and eyed the small tent that was suspended by a piece of twine strung from the front of the trailer to a spindly tree.

Inside the tent, Peter Sandler rolled over onto his stomach and propped himself up on his elbows. He flipped open his red notebook with *PETER'S LISTS* neatly printed in bold block letters on its cover. At the top of a fresh page he wrote *Horse show. July 10. I have to stay here* with Kim because Davey got sick and Mom had to rush home with him. The following list describes my feelings.

Next he numbered down the page from 1 to 26, a number for each letter of the alphabet. Beside 1 he wrote *Annoyed.* For 2 he put *Bored.* Then came *Cranky.* He had just finished printing *Disgusted* when Kim stuck her head in the other end of the tent.

"What are you doing in there?" she demanded as she pushed her bangs off her damp forehead.

"Nothin'."

"I don't believe you. I know you're making one of your idiotic lists. Please get out here and help me like Mom said you should. The costume class starts soon, and I've got to get Jewel ready and then change into my clown outfit and make up my face and everything."

There was just enough panic in her voice to make Peter listen, but not enough to spur him into action. Now what could he write for 5? he wondered.

"Hurry, Peter! Please!"

"I'm trying to think of something for the letter *E* that describes my mood," he said.

"*Enthusiastic!*" screeched Kim, grabbing his ankles and dragging him into the glaring noonday sun.

Peter blinked his eyes and ran his tongue along his parched lips. *Dehydrated,* he thought. That's what I should have used for *D.* "Kimmie, why do you come to these dumb shows?"

"Because they're fun!" she said fiercely. "Now where are those ribbons?" She was pawing through a heap of clothing on the ground next to the trailer.

"You know what your problem is?" Peter asked as he patted Jewel's sleek neck.

Kim grunted, "Yeah, you!"

"You're not organized," said Peter.

Kim hurled a clear plastic bag filled with narrow ribbons at her brother. "I am *so* organized. It's just that Mom usually helps out. Now start putting those ribbons in Jewel's mane."

"She isn't organized either."

"Not too many horses are," Kim said sarcastically through clenched teeth.

"If Mom was organized, she would have brought little bottles of orange juice and some raisins and nuts for Davey to eat. Then he wouldn't have had three doughnuts, two hot dogs, and four candy bars."

Kim wrinkled her nose. "He ate all that junk? No wonder he threw up. You're the one who kept taking him back to the snack bar. So this mess is all your fault."

"I was just trying to keep him out of your hair."

"Speaking of hair . . . put these ribbons in Jewel's. Now!"

Peter gave an injured sigh and set to work. He divided the mare's mane carefully into sections and slipped rubber bands around the ends. Then he began braiding. It was a neat, organized job, just the kind he enjoyed.

Kim was decorating Jewel's flowing flaxen tail. She glanced around the mare's side and said, "Hey, Pete, that looks good."

"These ribbons match Davey's tent," said Peter, waving a brilliant red one in Kim's direction.

"Yeah. They match my costume, too. Mom made the tent out of some extra material from my clown outfit. Oh, hurry up, Peter. It doesn't have to be perfect!"

"I thought you wanted to get a prize."

"Sure, but I won't. Didn't you notice cute little Barb Temblermen? She's got her pony all dolled up like a lamb, and she's Little Bo-Peep. And there must be at least three people with those incredible Arabian princess or sheik outfits with yards of fancy material and spangles and tassels. They always win."

"But you told Mom that this class was being judged partially on originality."

"It is. But I couldn't think of anything better than a clown, and that's just not that original. Now, where's Jewel's hat? Topaz!" Kim shrieked.

The colt jerked back as the girl lunged toward him. He had the brim of a floppy purple straw hat held firmly between his front teeth.

Peter grinned as he caught Topaz's halter and held him steady while Kim pried open his mouth and removed the hat.

"It's all wet! And look—teeth marks!" yelled Kim.

"Now that's original," said Peter, taking the hat. He placed it on Jewel's head and carefully pulled her ears through the holes made especially for that purpose.

Topaz looked up at his dam quizzically.

"Please keep an eye on these two while I get changed," Kim admonished breathlessly as she scrambled into the trailer, her makeshift dressing room.

Peter selected a soft-bristled brush and began to

groom Topaz. The colt's downy muddy-brown coat was beginning to shed out. Around his eyes and on his legs his coloring was showing a promise of someday fitting his name.

The announcer's voice suddenly blasted out over their heads. "Class number eight—Costume Class—should be ready to enter the ring in three minutes."

"Peter! Help me get up on Jewel," Kim said as she tumbled out of the trailer and stumbled toward her horse. "I can't mount with these fat pant legs."

"You look great." Peter offered his words of encouragement along with his clasped hands, which Kim used as a step to mount.

"Yikes! You didn't spray her back with Show Sheen, did you? I feel as if I'm gonna slide right off."

"No way." Peter shook his head emphatically. "It's probably the material in your clown suit."

"Just what I need," muttered Kim, "Slip-n-Slide pants. And I hope Topaz won't be too upset about his mom leaving him behind."

Peter looked up at his sister's face. The huge clown grin that was painted there did not match her anxious voice.

"Don't worry," he said with authority. "You take care of Jewel, and leave Topaz to Mr. Organization."

Another announcement boomed over their heads. "Costume Class may now enter from the south side of the ring."

"Good luck!" Peter called as Jewel and Kim trotted away. Then he took hold of Topaz's lead rope and firmly turned the colt's head away from the sight of his departing dam.

Topaz was not to be fooled. He let out a heart-wrenching whinny and began to prance in place. "Come on, baby," said Peter. "Don't look." He untied the colt and led him a few steps alongside the trailer, trying to hide his view. But the angle was wrong, and Topaz could still see his dam.

"I know," Peter muttered. He led Topaz to the open end of the tent and crawled inside. The colt dropped his head and sniffed curiously at the entrance. For the moment his mother was forgotten. He could not resist this opportunity to explore the strange structure he'd been staring at off and on all morning.

Peter held his cupped hand toward the colt's twitching nose. Topaz stuck his head inside and snorted at Peter's empty palm. He stepped forward hesitantly.

"That's a boy! Wow! I didn't think you'd actually come inside," said Peter. The colt sniffed the ground and then tried to lift his head. The tips of his ears bumped into the top of the tent.

He pulled back, but Peter was ready for him with strong tension on the lead rope. Topaz stretched out his neck and whinnied loudly.

"Ah, shut up!" wailed Peter. "There's hardly room for me in here without you and your loud mouth!"

Peter couldn't hear Jewel's whinny from the show ring, but her colt did. Topaz pranced forward one step and jammed his nose out the open triangular-shaped window near the top of the tent.

"Hey, you can't do that!"

But Topaz had his own ideas. He shoved his whole head outside and whinnied again.

Peter could see the colt's sides quiver, but the noise wasn't too bad. He hung on to the lead rope with a tight grip that turned into a stranglehold as Topaz stepped forward, straining against the fabric panel below the tent window. The twine at the top of the tent jerked up and down.

"Wait a sec," Peter muttered, struggling to his feet. But there was no room to stand.

Topaz lurched forward just as Peter's foot skidded on his open notebook. "Ouch!" Peter cried when a small hoof trampled his sneakered toe. He fell against the colt's side as he staggered to his full height. The tent bulged up above his head, and Peter tripped over the end of the lead rope. He grabbed for support and caught the twine at the top of the tent.

"Uh-oh," Peter said, just as the twine broke with a sharp snap.

Topaz could see and hear fine with his head sticking out the window of the tent. He called to his dam again and trotted around the end of the trailer toward the ring. There was Jewel, calling back to him incessantly.

Inside the tent, or what was left of it, Peter held on to the lead rope grimly with both hands. The small pegs that had held the sides of the tent to the ground had been pulled out and were flapping along next to Topaz's sides and Peter's legs, spurring the colt to trot faster.

Peter could see nothing except bright tent fabric and a bit of Topaz's sweaty back. But he was certain the colt was leading him toward the ring.

"Whoa! Easy, boy. You dummy! I thought you were halter-trained!"

Just as Topaz reached the opening to the ring, Peter stumbled and pitched onto the ground with a thud that knocked the breath out of his lungs and the rope out of his hands.

With a happy nicker of greeting, Topaz galloped across the ring toward Jewel. Peter staggered up and clung to the fence. Oh, boy, he thought, is Kimmie ever going to get me for this!

In the show ring, one of the Arabians shied away from the strange-looking colt. Little Bo-Peep shook her shepherdess's staff at him as he raced past. When Topaz reached Jewel's side, he skidded to a halt. Kim's mouth hung open, and Jewel stared at her foal.

The spectators, who were braving the shimmering heat of the metal bleachers, clapped and laughed at the colt dressed as a tent. The judge was laughing, too.

As if she were insulted by their rude reaction to her foal's predicament, Jewel shook her head. Then she reached down and grasped in her teeth the fabric covering Topaz's back. She pulled and tugged until there was a distinct sound of tearing cloth. Topaz backed out of the remains of his costume as Jewel let go of it. The mare and colt touched noses. Several cheers came from the stands.

Peter climbed through the fence rails. He walked

quickly over to Topaz, caught the trailing lead rope, and scooped the ragged tent from the ground. He started to lead the colt from the ring, but the judge smiled and motioned for him to line up beside Jewel in the center of the ring.

Peter wasn't surprised a moment later when the first-place ribbon was awarded to the most elaborately costumed Arabian princess on her elegant bay gelding.

"Second place," boomed the announcer, "goes to Kimberly Sandler on her mare, Jewel, and to . . . a . . . the little clown, too." A muffled chuckle came from the loudspeaker, and laughter and applause from the spectators.

"Third place . . ." But Peter wasn't listening. He grinned up at Kim and mouthed the word *Exuberant*. As they left the ring, Kim's expression matched her clown makeup perfectly.

After that day—and despite the fact that Topaz grew into a handsome horse with a glowing golden-brown coat befitting his name—Peter and Kim always called him just plain "Clown."

HORSE SENSE

She couldn't see. Even when Janelle stood on tiptoe, the list attached to the bulletin board was completely hidden by a huge cluster of campers.

"You gotta be kiddin'! Look who he gave me," one boy complained. "He knows I hate Comet."

As a few campers moved away from the board, some grumbling, some grinning, Janelle squeezed closer.

"Hey, who'd you get?" called a voice.

Janelle shook her head without turning toward Marcie. "Don't know yet."

"Coming through!" Marcie said in her loud, assertive voice, and she shoved right past the other campers, including Janelle. "Hey, you got Rusty," she announced a second later. "Why'd he give you that ol' nag? You think he's telling me what I've known all along—that

I'm the better rider?" Marcie's tone was light and teasing, but Janelle knew that beneath the surface she meant what she said.

Janelle shrugged. "I guess Daniel knows what he's doing." But she was disappointed. Why had the riding instructor assigned her to Rusty for the last major event of the camp season, a long trail ride through the woods and countryside?

"Guess who I got," demanded Marcie.

"Who cares?" was Janelle's mumbled reply.

"Slicker! Funny, huh? I got the best, and you got the worst."

Janelle could picture the two horses clearly: Slicker, the sleek chestnut with aristocratic Thoroughbred looks and clean white blaze, and next to him, Rusty, the dumpy-looking bay with the mane that never would lie flat . . .

"Tin Can! That's what they should call him instead of Rusty," said Marcie with an artificial giggle. "He's just a piece of junk. We pay a fortune to come here, and they keep trash like him around to make us ride. Boy, I feel sorry for you."

"Yeah, I bet," said Janelle.

There was a sharp, bitter edge to the two girls' rivalry. Although this was Janelle's first season at Echo Hill Camp, she'd had riding lessons from the time she was old enough to hold the reins. Starting with the first day at camp, she had been aware of Marcie watching her in riding class, judging, comparing, finding fault —but not enough fault.

Because Janelle had confidence in her riding ability, she had been able to ignore Marcie, until the other girl's simmering resentment boiled over into additional areas of camp life. They were the same age and shared a cabin with eight other girls and a counselor. This arrangement provided Marcie with access to Janelle's belongings.

One day Janelle couldn't find her swimsuit. It was only luck that one of the younger campers discovered it draped over some bushes when he sneaked off into the woods to use a tree for a rest stop.

Another time, when Janelle shoved her feet into her sneakers, she noticed they felt more damp than she'd expected. But she was in a hurry to get ready for the hike, and she put them on without checking inside. Halfway up the long climb to the summit of Echo Hill, she stopped to rest and tried to take off her shoes. Her socks were stuck to her shoes, and her feet were stuck to her socks.

Marcie's fit of snickering clued everyone in to the culprit. When they got back to camp, Janelle had to soak her feet, sneakers and all, in warm water for twenty minutes to loosen the glue enough to extricate her sore toes. Afterwards, she confronted Marcie, demanding that she stop being such a pest. But Marcie just giggled and said sweetly, "Can't you take a joke? You're so sensitive! I guess you just don't understand. This is all part of camp—you know, tradition."

Later Janelle's best friend, Roberta, said, "You gotta get her back! *That's* tradition. Come on, I know. We'll jello her bed. We'll use that awful green stuff that the cook keeps giving us for Friday desserts. Marcie'll look like the Creature with the Green Crud when she hops out. That'll fix her!"

"No," said Janelle.

But the temptation to retaliate grew greater the day they were all eating dinner at Cabin 3's table, and Marcie dropped her fork on the floor.

"Hey, get that," she ordered Janelle.

"Get it yourself. You're closer."

"Oh, sorry," said Marcie with artificial sincerity. "I really am. For just a sec I thought you were Veronica."

Janelle did not take the bait, but one of the other girls asked, "Who's she?"

"Our maid," replied Marcie with a small grin. "I must've thought I was at home."

"Yeah," said Roberta. "What a shame your manners are just as bad here as there!"

Janelle felt her face growing hot as she stared at her plate during the embarrassed silence that followed the exchange between Marcie and Roberta. She finally glanced up and around at the girls' faces. Marcie was the only one who seemed comfortable, leaning back on her chair nonchalantly with the remains of a smirk on her lips.

That night Roberta said, "Marcie's a creep. Let's take all the slats out of her bunk."

"What about Pat? She sleeps on the bottom bunk. And she always goes to bed before Marcie."

"Excuses! What's with you? Don't you want to pound her into the ground? Really, Janelle, she deserves it!"

Janelle nodded. "Yeah, I know, and I do."

But Janelle knew exactly where her parents stood on such matters. They hadn't sent her to camp to get into a fight. She could almost hear her mother saying "Don't stoop to her level."

So instead of helping Roberta think up interesting methods of revenge, Janelle had channeled her anger and energy that summer into improving her riding skills. Daniel was a good instructor, and she knew she was learning more in these few months than she had in the last several years. He had a way of helping her understand a horse.

"Riding is more than just sitting up there, *making* a horse do what you want," he told his students. "They've got feelings, too. Horse sense, if you know what I mean. You and your horse are a team."

Daniel insisted that the older and better riders switch horses instead of riding the same one day after day, as the young children usually did. He said this helped his students learn to understand each horse as an individual.

But Rusty? Marcie was right about him; he did act like an ol' nag.

Now Janelle stared after Marcie as she dashed off to brag about Slicker to some other girls. The crowd at the bulletin board had thinned out, so Janelle skirted the remaining campers to look at the list herself. It would be just like Marcie to pretend Janelle had been assigned ol' Rusty Tin Can when actually Daniel had given her an excellent horse.

But Marcie had not been lying.

There were the names in clear black ink, side by side: *Janelle/Rusty.*

Disappointment pinched her lips tight. It wasn't fair! She'd hardly ever even ridden Rusty. Usually he was saved for the younger kids or those with very little riding experience. And even with them, he could be obstreperous— not cantering when commanded, refusing to jump, tossing his head when they were supposed to be standing still.

Janelle took a long, deep, deliberate breath. She knew that without Marcie's snide comments, she would not be so upset. She was sure that Daniel was not being mean. All summer he'd treated her fairly and with respect, and she wasn't about to go whining to him now about getting the "wrong" horse. Besides, Daniel had made it perfectly clear that his assignments were carefully thought out and that his mind could not be changed.

"Hey, Janelle! I see you got Rusty. He's not so bad." It was Roberta, standing beside her with a huge grin on her face. "I got Caramel! She's great! She's my favorite. Did you see the way she jumped for me in that last class?"

Janelle smiled and nodded, trying to be glad for her friend. But somewhere inside, she felt tired and defeated. It seemed that the undeclared war between Marcie and her had ended before she'd even decided to join the battle.

And Marcie was the winner.

"Listen up!" Daniel's commanding voice cut through the creak of saddles and the clink of bits.

It was the next morning, and the air was saturated with moisture. Fog nestled in the trees, cloaking the familiar campground in a mysterious disguise. Every blade of grass was bent over with its burden of heavy mist.

"Here's the lineup," Daniel continued. "You've all got to stay in your assigned places. Single file. The ground's slippery, so let's be careful. First horse, Rusty. Second, Caramel. Third, Blaze . . ."

Janelle moved Rusty up into position. He stepped lightly over a puddle and pricked his ears alertly. She patted his neck. He felt different than she remembered from the few times she'd ridden him in the ring. More collected, maybe. More interested.

Janelle couldn't help smiling to herself, thinking that Daniel would be pleased because she was actually getting in tune with her horse. She felt as if she could read Rusty's mind, understand his feelings. She could sense a gathering of pride in his arched neck and quick snort; he seemed to be aware of the honor of having been chosen to lead the trail ride.

There was no doubt in her mind—Rusty preferred being out of that boring riding ring. Janelle sat up straight and collected the reins in firm hands.

"Larry!" called Daniel. "You ride real calm and steady. Blaze doesn't like those puddles. Notice how he's staring at them?"

"Okay, sure," muttered Larry.

"All set?" asked Daniel.

There was a chorus of yeses, and then he gave the signal to start forward.

Rusty stepped confidently along the sodden path, undeterred by mud or puddles.

When the trail sloped, Janelle leaned back slightly to help her horse balance on the slippery terrain. This was fun! Out here in front, it was almost as if they were alone, separate, just the two of them, exploring a new, foreign land of shadowy tree trunks and soft gray mist.

She hummed softly to drown out the voices of the other campers and patted Rusty's neck. She was only vaguely aware of Larry yelling at Blaze or Roberta squealing each time a wet branch brushed her face.

As the trail made a turn to the left, Janelle peered ahead, squinting and concentrating on the faint sound coming from beyond the retreating barrier of fog. Rusty's ears swiveled forward, and she knew he was listening, too. Quite suddenly Janelle realized that they were hearing the rushing gurgle of the creek, which must have been enlarged by the recent rain.

The path leveled off and began to follow the creek, but the suspended moisture was even thicker, and Janelle could see nothing beyond the trunks of trees that grew along the top of the bank.

"Can't we go any faster?" asked Larry.

"No," came Daniel's quick and decisive reply from far back at the end of the line. "Rusty's setting the pace."

"I'm falling asleep," another camper whined.

"Things'll improve in a few minutes," said Daniel.

"Janelle! Take the next right fork in the trail."

Janelle called, "Okay." Then she watched closely so she wouldn't miss the spot where the trail split. She reined Rusty to the right, and almost immediately, the trail dropped away in front of them, directly down the steep embankment to the muddy, rapidly flowing creek.

"Hey!" Roberta yelled. "That's too deep!"

"No, it's not," said Daniel authoritatively. "I rode out this morning to check it, and it's only a bit higher than usual. You won't even have to pull up your feet."

"I should hope not," Marcie commented. "Wouldn't want to get my good boots wet."

Halfway down the slope, his haunches pulled up beneath him, Rusty braced his front hooves and stopped. He gazed intently at the water, swung his head to look upstream, and drew in his breath with a rattly snort.

Janelle stared across the creek at the mist-shrouded trees and underbrush. One section looked like some sort of crouching creature, half dissolving in ghostly gray, a giant troll waiting to collect its victims as they crossed over. For the first time, Janelle felt a twinge of apprehension.

The line of horses nudged closer, but Rusty stood firm, his feet sliding slightly in the mud.

"Now what?" Larry demanded impatiently.

Janelle could feel Rusty's body gathered tautly beneath her as she tried to press him forward with a steady tightening of both her legs. He lurched one more step downward, then refused to budge. Janelle thought she sensed a slight tremor in his body, almost like a shiver.

"Give him a kick," advised Daniel from way back. He sounded a bit annoyed.

"Janelle, you think you're such a hotshot rider," muttered Larry, "but even you can't get that dumb nag across a stupid creek."

"Shall I let Caramel bite his rear end?" asked Roberta with a giggle.

"Rusty's an ol' pro at crossing water," called Daniel. "Just be firm."

Janelle tried to relax. Maybe Rusty felt some hesitation on her part, because she didn't like the looks of the woods or the creek either. But there was no real reason for concern; Daniel knew what he was doing. That was his job. And, actually, she could see from here that the water was only a little above its normal level. This creek consisted of the spillover from the placid pond that the camp used for teaching canoeing skills. There was nothing to fear.

She took a careful breath and calmed her hands.

"Hey, Daniel," said Marcie. "Want me to go around and take the lead? I'm sure I can get Slicker to cross."

A wave of resentment washed hotly over Janelle's face, but she bit her tongue and concentrated on getting her horse across the creek.

She pressed against his sides again and poked him with her heels, but this time Rusty's resistance was unmistakable. He tossed his head and turned it, looking for an escape.

It was just as if Rusty were talking to her. The urge to force him to obey suddenly left her. If her horse was talking, it was her job to listen. And without a doubt he was saying "No!" to crossing the creek.

"We have to go back!" Janelle said with determination.

"Ah, come on," grumbled Larry.

"Daniel, this is ridiculous," came Marcie's exasperated, superior voice.

But just then another camper let out a frightened squawk, and someone else screeched, "What's *that?*"

Janelle felt fear prick like a knife blade at the back of her neck.

Daniel yelled, "About-face!"

Rusty was already turning, not waiting for Janelle's response to the command. He staggered and scrambled up alongside Caramel and Roberta.

He knew, just as Janelle did, what was coming toward them, right around that bend and beyond the misty trees, through the fog, roaring with fury and power.

Water!

"Come on!" Janelle cried, catching a glimpse of Roberta's terrified face.

"The dam broke!" yelled Daniel. "Get going!"

Rusty stumbled down onto one knee as he lurched up the bank. Janelle toppled forward, nearly unseated, and grasped a fistful of mane as the horse managed to regain his footing and leap to level ground. One rein dangled too long, and as Janelle started to gather it up, Rusty bounded across the path and galloped into the woods, leaving the crash and turmoil of the flash flood behind.

Twigs and branches and soaking wet leaves smashed into Janelle's face and tore her legs. She leaned close to Rusty's neck, where damp strands of mane whipped her cheeks.

"Easy, boy," she whispered as she pulled back, and Rusty slowed to a trot, then a walk. Janelle looked around at the trees and brush that surrounded them. In the dense mist beyond their protective walls, she could hear the sounds of other horses galloping and riders shrieking.

"Whoa, there!" That was Daniel's voice, trying to stop the runaways and restore order.

Janelle rubbed Rusty's neck and hummed softly to him, reassuring herself and her horse. It was as if they had escaped to their own private world, and they were in no hurry to leave it. She took a shaky breath and noticed the scent of crushed leaves and moist earth.

"Help! Ouch!" screamed someone nearby.

Janelle turned Rusty in the direction of the cries, and he picked his way through the underbrush and over fallen logs toward the sound.

"Ow! Ow! I'm hurt. Help!"

They found Marcie standing next to a thicket, her jacket sleeve in shreds and her arm scratched.

"What happened?" asked Janelle sympathetically.

"What do you think?" said Marcie, spitting the words in fury. "That idiot horse crashed me into a tree . . . or a wall or something. I hate Slicker!"

Janelle dismounted to examine Marcie's arm. The cut looked minor, but she kept moaning dramatically. She asked bitterly, "Where is everybody else? I'm hurt—where's Daniel?"

"He's got his hands full," said Janelle. "We'd better head back to the path. I'm sure Rusty can find it. Come on. We can ride double. Rusty won't mind."

"Double? With *you?*" said Marcie.

Janelle looked directly into the other girl's wide green eyes. She shook her head slightly, then said slowly and very clearly, "Yeah, with *me*. Unless you'd rather walk."

Marcie hesitated for a long moment before she muttered in a tone that was a mixture of gratitude and defeat, "Okay. Double."

A HORSE FOR ALL SEASONS

– AUTUMN –

BROTHERS

When school starts in a couple of days, I'm going to be prepared. I don't mean notebook and pens and a green eraser. I'm talking *Prepared* with a capital *P*.

Ever since I was in third grade at Cedarfield Elementary School I've had the same assignment the first week: "Write a story about your summer vacation." I'm in junior high now, but I bet my English teacher will tell us to do it, too.

The only thing harder than writing one of those stories is listening to the other kids read theirs. Let's face it, Cedarfield is not the most exciting place to live. Last year I wrote about the stray dog who had her puppies under my bed. My teacher, Mrs. Brinderhoff, wanted to know why a stray was in our house. So I started to tell her about how we'd heard the dog howling outside, and since it was cold and rainy, my brother Rory and I had brought her in. Mrs. Brinderhoff just handed my paper back to me. She said, "Write it, Seth. Don't tell me with your mouth. Use your pen."

Anyhow, as I was saying (with my pen), Cedarfield is sort of *Dull* with a capital *D*. My dad always says we're a bunch of good, honest farmers. Dull.

Dad likes it here, though, and I guess Rory and I do, too. Rory's two years older than me, and we look a lot alike. People are constantly asking if we're twins. We've always lived here on our farm six miles northeast of Cedarfield, just the three of us since our mom died when Rory and I were real little. I can't remember her much. I like to look at all the old snapshots of her riding her horse, Golden Lass. We still have Goldie. She's real old now.

Rory and I learned to ride on Goldie when we were tiny. But now we've got our own horses. They're full brothers, Goldie's sons. Their sire is Jake Samuels's big chestnut quarter horse, Fancy Fortune.

Copper is my horse, and he looks like his name. He's one year younger than me, which makes him eleven. He's almost 16 hands high. That means from the ground up to his withers (the spot where his neck joins his back) he's that tall. Each "hand" is the same as 4 inches. (Mrs. Brinderhoff always said to include details.) Bronze belongs to Rory. He looks as much like Copper as I look like Rory.

A couple of summers ago we entered a bunch of horse shows, and the only class where we won the blue ribbon was called "matched pairs." Even though Bronze went on the wrong lead twice, we were sure matched.

Showing was kind of fun. But Rory and I like other sorts of competition more. We're always trying to beat each other at something. Dad says, "Can't you boys ever cooperate?" I don't know how he expects us to cooperate when we're playing Monopoly or video games or racing our horses.

Every time we go off riding, Dad tells us to be careful. So we are—careful to make sure he doesn't see us racing. Copper is faster than Bronze. I think. But since Rory cheats and wins most of the time, I'm not sure.

Anyhow, last Tuesday started out like any other day. Rory and me, we'd been trying to get off for some fun for about a week. I mean, we knew school would be starting soon, and we were tired of working. Even riding can be work on a farm. We have 316 acres, and we rent another 240. When Dad makes us check fences it takes hours, and it's not much fun. Sure, we try to make a game of it, like we're Sioux looking over the white settlers, stuff like that. But most of the time it's just *Work* with a capital *W.*

That day we'd been helping Dad stack hay and haul it to a neighbor's place. They've got a bunch of horses, so they use square bales. Actually, the bales are rectangular-shaped. Dad makes great big round bales, too. Those we feed to our livestock. We have Angus cattle. They're fat and black. In a field they look like dark, squarish boulders. Until they move.

By the time Rory and I headed out to the horse

pasture on Tuesday, the sun was settling down into the trees off over Quarry Hill. So we knew we didn't have lots of time left before dark.

I whistled for Copper. I have a funny, shrill whistle, and Rory tells me I sound like a girl. But I don't care, because Copper always comes tearing over to me. Bronze just ignores Rory no matter how loud he whistles or calls.

"Here they come!" I said, even before we could see them. I had an eye on Cloudy, our dog, the one who had puppies under the bed.

She had stopped snuffling in the grass and was staring at a spot on the crest of the hill. Sure enough, Copper and then Bronze appeared. They swept down the hill and pulled up in front of the gate, nostrils all wide and flaring.

I gave Cloudy a pat on the head. She danced around us, barking hysterically.

"Shut your trap," ordered Rory. She didn't obey. Barking and chasing cattle every which way are Cloudy's favorite pastimes. Dad locks her up whenever he moves the cattle. She's okay when we're riding—the horses ignore her completely.

Rory climbed over the gate, and I followed.

"You using a saddle?" I asked.

He shook his head, and I frowned. Copper has one little fault. He bucks. Not all the time. Just when he's racing, and especially when he's catching up. He's okay if we've been riding for a long time. Or if I've got the saddle, there's no problem. But it gets a little tricky bareback.

That's one of the ways Rory cheats. He knows I won't admit that I need a saddle. When he rides bareback, I do, too. Then, when we race, I have to pull Copper's head up to make him stop bucking, which slows him down. So Bronze wins.

Another way Rory cheats is calling a race when I'm not ready. I was watching him very carefully now as we jogged along the trail that skirts the west edge of our property. We were in part of the cattle pasture that extends right across three hills and includes the 100-acre woods. I didn't think Rory would call a race now because Dad had driven a tractor and wagon here last week soon after a rainstorm, and there were some bad ruts dried in the trail. But I could never be sure about Rory. He's not the cautious type.

"All the cattle must be in the woods," Rory said.

I squinted out over the field and couldn't see any sign of the herd. By this time Cloudy, running full tilt, was way ahead of us.

"The herd's probably hiding from Cloudy." I whistled for her, and she came loping back and gave me a what-do-you-want look.

"It's okay," I told her. "Go ahead and chase rabbits." She took off, her white tail waving along like a flag.

The woods is my favorite part of the farm. With the cattle grazing in it, there's not much underbrush. But the trees have thick trunks and are close together, making it dense and secretive. When I was little, I thought it was the same Hundred Acre Wood that's in the Winnie-the-Pooh stories.

There's a trail in the woods that winds through the trees. We use it as a shortcut across our land to one of the county roads.

"Hurry up, Seth. It's getting dark," said Rory.

He was right. As we entered the thick woods, it was like stepping into a cave. But our eyes adjusted quickly, and we could see the trail stretched out in front of us, still pale like the sky.

"Remember when we used to pretend to go back in time?" Rory asked me.

"Sure." I nodded. With so few houses around, it's easy to imagine it's a hundred years ago.

"Seth, look at Cloudy. She's way up there."

I could barely see her, a wisp of silvery cloud floating where the trail met the dark woods beyond.

"Cloudy, stay!" I called.

"Readysetgo!" Rory shouted. "Race ya to Cloudy!"

They took off, leaving me and Copper just gathering ourselves together.

I grabbed Copper's mane as he leaped after his brother. With the wind and mane whipping my face, I couldn't see much except the rear end of Bronze.

I didn't dare kick Copper or try to slap him with my hand. I had my legs clamped into his sides, and my hands were really busy hanging on to the reins and his mane.

"Charge," I said urgently.

We were gaining! I could feel Copper stretching out beneath me. Now we were swerving around Bronze. Almost next to him and Rory . . . overtaking them!

Abruptly, Copper's head dropped lower, and I felt

the beginning of a buck in his arching back. I gave the reins a quick tug. Bronze tore ahead.

Falling off was forgotten—winning was all I wanted. I gave Copper a jab in both sides with my heels and let out a war whoop.

The combination worked.

Copper shot forward as if he'd been standing still. We passed Bronze, a blur on our left. I pressed against Copper's straining neck, the shadowy woods rushing by us on either side. I wanted to run like this forever.

Where's Cloudy? I wondered as we tore over the top of the slope. I was sure this was about where she'd been standing when I'd told her to stay. I pulled back, and Copper braced his front legs and slid his back ones beneath him as he stopped. Rory trotted up next to us.

I couldn't help gloating. "He tried to buck, and we still won!"

"Shut up. Listen."

For a second I thought Rory was just being a sore loser. Then I heard it, too: Cloudy, barking wildly.

"Bet she treed a 'coon," I said.

"Come on." Rory loped off around a bend in the trail.

I took my time, savoring the win. I patted Copper's neck and held him down to a slow jog.

In just a few seconds we met Rory and Bronze coming back toward us. Rory's face looked strangely pale in the gathering darkness.

"Something's wrong." He was almost whispering. "I heard some men's voices, and a bunch of our cattle are up ahead by the gate that opens onto Pond Road."

"So?" I said.

Rory motioned for me to follow him off the trail into the woods.

As the trees closed in around us, I shivered. I felt like a shadow was crawling under my shirt.

"Rustlers," whispered Rory.

I grinned. "Come on, Rory. Stop kidding around. We haven't gone back in time."

Cloudy's frantic barks tied us firmly to the here and now.

"Don't you remember what happened over near Jacobstown? About forty head of cattle stolen?" Rory asked in an urgent whisper.

I stopped grinning. "That's the next county," I said lamely.

"Here, you hold Bronze," Rory said as he slid off and tossed the reins to me.

"What're you doing?"

"Taking a closer look. I'll go over by the road, through the woods, and crawl under the fence. There's enough brush to hide me, but I should be able to see what's going on."

After Rory left, I just sat there while Copper and Bronze sniffed noses. It didn't seem to bother them at all to be standing around in the woods with night coming on real fast. They were content just being together, best friends as well as brothers.

There are lots of times when I'd just as soon not have a brother at all. But right then, sitting on my horse alone, I wished he'd come back—fast. Questions started to jump around in my brain. What if Cloudy heard him and gave away his hiding place? What if the rustlers kidnapped him, and I never saw him again? What if he was just playing a big joke on me?

"Hi," said Rory.

I jerked in surprise. "Why'd you sneak up behind me?" I demanded.

"I got lost. It's pretty dark here in the woods, but on the road I could see fine. There're two guys. They've got a stock trailer backed up against the gate. I think they've got some cattle loaded already. From the sounds of it, Cloudy's messing things up for them. You know how she is. You go get Dad. We'll need the cops. Hurry up! Don't just sit there!" Rory said all this in such a rush, his words tumbled over one another.

"What about you?"

"I'm going to try to get even closer. Maybe get a license number or something. Just go, Seth. Copper's faster than Bronze. Go!"

I hesitated. "The horses are going to whinny to each other, you know. What if the rustlers hear them?"

Rory shook his head. "With the racket Cloudy's making, they won't hear anything else."

"Okay," I said. "Be careful."

"You, too," he said as he tied Bronze's reins to a low branch.

I twirled Copper around and took off for the race home. We loped on the trail a short distance; then I decided to take a shortcut and plunged into the woods. There we slowed to a jog. I had to squint to see, and even then I got socked in the face with twigs a couple of times. I was relieved when we came to the creek. It was like a guiding path, shimmering with reflected moonlight. By following it, we made our way out of the woods and into the pasture. There I urged Copper into a gallop. This was familiar territory for him, and he flattened out into a dead run.

When we reached the driveway, I pulled Copper up and jumped off as he was sliding to a halt.

"Dad! Dad! Come quick!"

He came out the door and down the steps in one bound. I knew right away he thought Rory had gotten hurt.

"Rustlers!" I said quickly, resting against Copper's sweaty side. "Rory's okay. They're over on Pond Road where the gate is."

Dad didn't waste time or words. He rushed back inside the house while I walked Copper to the paddock and released him. I knew he'd wander around and cool himself off. I rubbed behind his ears and let him nuzzle my shoulder.

"Seth! Come on!"

Dad was already in the pickup with the motor running when I hopped in beside him.

"I called Jim Patterson, and he's heading over from his place," Dad told me as we tore out onto the road. "And someone from the sheriff's department will be coming out from town."

"Maybe the rustlers are gone by now," I said.

Dad drove like crazy until we hit Pond Road. There he turned off the headlights and slowed down. When we were almost at the gate, he let the truck coast down one hill and gave it just enough gas to climb the next.

I held my breath.

At the top of the hill Dad turned on the high beams. We roared down and slammed to a stop about ten feet in front of the other pickup.

"You fellows lost or something?" Dad asked really slow and loud while he stepped out of the truck.

I slithered down and peered over the dashboard.

Two men were standing next to their stock trailer, blinking at the headlights. Cloudy was still barking hoarsely.

Jim Patterson pulled up on the other side of the rustlers' truck and climbed out with a shotgun in his hands.

"Some problem here, neighbor?" he called.

"No, not anymore, Jim," said Dad. "These gentlemen are going to stand right here until the police arrive. You're welcome to join me while I keep them company."

Gentlemen? I thought.

"Shut up!" one of the rustlers yelled. "Idiot dog! My head's killin' me."

Cloudy came bounding along through the woods. I could just make her out, a white chalk smear against the dark foliage. But I could hear her just fine. The cattle had all scattered, so now she was yapping at Bronze and Rory.

"Hey, Seth!" Rory called, waving from the far side of the gate. The rustlers glared at him.

I slid cautiously out of the pickup.

Cloudy hurled herself through the gate and dashed over. Panting and whining, she flung herself at my feet.

"Fool dog," Dad remarked mildly.

Jim Patterson laughed. "That's some cow dog you've got there."

"She earned her keep tonight," Dad said, grinning.

"Yeah," grumbled a rustler with a sarcastic snort.

Just then the police car arrived, and it was all over. Almost.

After the rustlers were taken away, we put the cattle from the stock trailer back into our woods. I shut Cloudy in the pickup so she wouldn't try to help. No point in ruining a good thing.

Jim gave Rory and me each a slap on the back and told us, "You boys did quite a job."

"Thanks for being a one-man posse," Dad told him before he drove off.

"Hey, Seth. You going home with Dad or me?" asked Rory.

"With you," Dad decided. "You can keep each other out of trouble." He boosted me up on Bronze behind Rory.

"Don't cut through the woods," Dad continued. "It's too dark, despite the moon. Take your time. I'll check on Copper and water him soon as I get home."

We were halfway home when I asked Rory, "Did you mean it about Copper being faster?"

I felt Rory's shoulders shrug in front of me. "Maybe. Or maybe I just wanted you to go get Dad. I'm older, and watching rustlers is dangerous business."

I kind of laughed, remembering those rustlers and Cloudy and everything. That's when I knew I was prepared. I had my story for the first day of school.

"What's so funny?" asked Rory.

"Ah, you know. Cloudy and stuff."

"Right," Rory said. A comfortable silence folded around us like the darkness. When we reached our driveway Bronze whinnied a loud greeting. Copper answered from the paddock.

Brothers with a capital *B*.

HAUNTED HAYRIDE

"Where'd you get all these briers, Peaches? I should've made you stay in your stall all day." With a disgusted sigh, Alice plucked at the snarl of prickly, dry vegetation in the horse's mane.

"Here, try the dog brush," offered Cindy. "It works better than the mane comb."

Dustin lay sprawled in the large horse manger, watching his older sisters groom the pair of Belgians. He chewed lazily on a stalk of hay, savoring the sweet taste of summer that it brought into the October-chilled barn.

"Hey, look at Cricket!" said Alice. "I bet she's jealous. Sorry, sweetie. No barrel races today." The trim black mare continued to lean against the bottom half of her stall door. Her dark eyes followed the girls' every movement.

"Scoot over, Cream." Cindy shoved at the horse's massive side, and the docile animal stepped sideways.

"How come you're makin' such a fuss?" asked Dustin, waving the hay like a pointer at his sisters. "It's gonna be too dark for anybody to see if they're covered with muck."

"No, it won't. Better not be. Dad'll make us call off the hayride if the moon isn't out," said Alice.

"But you don't want it *too* light," said Cindy with a grin.

"Oh, shut up," Alice answered good-naturedly, her already pink cheeks blushing darker.

Dustin struggled into a different position. Was that vague tickle a splinter working its way through the seat of his jeans? He decided to ignore it. "So, Mick's comin' on the hayride?" he asked.

"Sure," Alice said nonchalantly.

"If you've invited boys, how come Ted and me can't come, too?"

"Ted and *I*," corrected Cindy.

"*You're* already going," said Dustin. "You're driving the team."

"Stop being a smart mouth," Cindy retorted. The oldest of the three, at sixteen, she often acted more like a parent than a sibling.

Alice planted her hands on her hips and scowled at Dustin. "I'll tell you why you can't come. You guys are too immature."

"We'll bring some cute girls along and show you how mature we can be," countered Dustin.

"This is *my* party, Dustin! No way are you gettin' on that wagon." Alice was beginning to have that frantic look that Dustin always found amusing. He grinned impishly.

"Stop that!" yelled Alice.

"Okay, okay. I promise I won't get on your stupid wagon. Who'd want to ride through the woods with a bunch of kissin' high school jerks?" With that comment, he squirmed from the manger and trotted out the barn door. "Besides," he called back. "Ted and *me* are having pizza and watching blood-curdling movies on the VCR."

A stiff autumn breeze rattled the brown leaves of the oak in the yard. Dustin glanced up at the gnarled branches as he sprinted past it. Once he'd tried to climb that tree and gotten stuck—not a pleasant memory. But that was years ago. Now he knew how to plan his adventures. This past week he and Ted had spent several hours making arrangements for tonight.

At the back stoop he found Jessica, the old black Lab, slumped on the doormat. He paused to scratch under her chin. She lifted her graying muzzle and gazed up at him with clouded eyes.

"You want to come along with us tonight? It's gonna be the best adventure ever!" The dog waved her tail at the tone in his voice. "I don't know—you'd probably have trouble keeping up. But you can watch the movie."

The door opened a crack and Dustin's father said, "Telephone for you."

Jessica followed Dustin into the kitchen, where his mother was scurrying around preparing for the party. As Dustin picked up the phone, his mom asked his dad, "Are you sure we've got enough potato chips and pretzels and dip?"

Over the growl of his stomach, Dustin said, "Hello?"

"Hey, Dusty, it's me."

"Teddy Boy, what's up?"

"Nothin'. That's the problem. I can't come."

"What!" Dustin pulled the phone cord as far into the living room as it could go and leaned against the wall. "Why not? I need you!"

"It's not my fault. Remember when my stupid cousins came to visit a couple weeks ago? Well, the little one, the one who kept shooting our cats with his water pistol—cute little Chippy—he got chicken pox the next day. Guess who caught 'em from him."

"Chicken pox? Are you kidding? That's baby stuff!"

"Tell me about it!" said Ted. "I tried convincing my mom the spots were zits, but she didn't believe me. And I've got a fever and everything. She's making me go to bed."

Dustin groaned. "I thought we had it planned just perfect. I won't go without you and Charcoal. I need another horse to make Cricket behave."

"She's just a horse. Alice rides her all the time," said Ted. "You can do it, Dusty. I'm going to be thinking about you all night. I have to have something to keep my mind off these spots. They itch!"

Dustin stared out the window at the graying sky. The

hayride would be starting soon. "Okay. I'll try it. For you, Teddy. I'll call you tomorrow and tell you all about it."

The next half hour Dustin spent in his bedroom readying his equipment. He had safety-pinned an old dark blanket into a crude cape the night before. Now he shoved it in his duffel bag on top of two tubes of makeup, a flashlight, and an old plastic sword.

"All set, Jessie," he told the dog, who had trailed him to his room. "Hear that? Here come the first guests." He peered out his window and settled down to wait until several more of Alice's friends had arrived and were climbing into the wagon.

"Let's go!" said Dustin. The old dog staggered off his bed and followed him down to the kitchen, where Dustin heaped a paper plate with food before clumping down the stairs to the basement rec room.

In the small bathroom, Dustin carefully applied white and black makeup. He drew dark rings around his eyes and filled them in. The effect was satisfyingly ghoulish.

"What do you think?" he asked Jessica, who was making herself comfortable on top of his sleeping bag. She gave one thump of her tail. "Okay, so you're not overwhelmed. I'll look better in the woods. Move over. I've got to arrange you so you can be my substitute."

Dustin bunched the sleeping bag and blankets around the dog so that just the back of her head was toward the stairway. Then he put the videotape in the VCR and turned up the volume.

"There. If Mom peeks down, she'll think I'm here."

He hunched into the makeshift cape and left the house by the steps that led directly out of the basement to the yard. Several cobwebs caught on his face, but he told himself any ghoul would enjoy the creepy sensation.

He left the basement door propped open and peered around the corner of the house. The horse team was just starting to pull the wagon onto the trail.

With cape flying, Dustin dashed across the yard to the barn.

Cricket had gone out into the paddock, but he managed to lure her into her stall with a pail of oats. She took quick grabs of the grain, while watching him suspiciously with white-ringed eyes.

"Come on, Cricket," Dustin pleaded. "It's going to be fun. We're in this together. I need you tonight. Without you, I can't catch up with the hayride." All the while he saddled and bridled the skittish horse, Dustin kept talking. "I've ridden you before . . . a couple of times. We'll do great, you and me." He hoped he sounded more confident than he felt.

The cape had begun to prickle around his neck, and twice he tripped over the end of it. He rubbed his sweaty face and then wiped the smeary makeup onto his jeans.

Cricket finished her oats and looked at Dustin with an expression that could only be called a glare.

"Well, here goes," he muttered, jamming his flashlight into a back pocket. He led Cricket out into the barnyard and swung into the saddle. His sword fit neatly in a belt loop.

"Ouch!" said Dustin. Yes, there was definitely a splinter somewhere in the saddle area. He wished he were riding Peaches or Cream. With one of them he wouldn't need a saddle; he'd welcome that wide, cushiony back. But he needed Cricket's speed to carry him parallel to the hayride and cut in front of it. He figured that the wagon had left about fifteen minutes before, and the team was now ambling along the path beside the stream and into the woods. Dustin's plan was to gallop in the field beside the woods and overtake them.

As they entered the partially harvested, moonlit cornfield, Cricket snorted and swung her head from side to side. She eyed with alarm the stalks of dried corn that stood like skeletons of their former selves. The wind sent the dead leaves into a frenzy of rustling, like the clicking of miniature bones. Dustin pressed his heels into the mare's sides, but she refused to move faster than a nervous prance.

Glancing at his illuminated watch, Dustin sighed loudly. "Come on, you ol' nag. I thought you were a racehorse."

Suddenly the cornstalks to their right erupted as a bird flung itself into the night air. Cricket bolted.

Dustin slipped to one side, and his cape loosened and flapped over Cricket's rump with an angry crack. The mare ran with fear and fury as Dustin struggled to regain his precarious perch.

He clutched the saddle horn and gradually righted himself. Cricket stretched out and tore along in the open section of field that was like a channel between rows of corn.

Dustin began to haul back on the reins. He muttered "Turn, you stupid horse" as he attempted to slow her down. Finally she dropped into a lope and then a fast jog that bounced Dustin high out of the saddle. He managed to steer her out of the field and toward the woods.

"Look!" he almost shouted as he glimpsed the light of the wagon lantern twinkling momentarily between tree trunks. "We made it! We got ahead of them." Dustin reached down and stroked Cricket's warm neck.

He urged the mare into the undergrowth at the edge of the woods. Then she plunged on into the woods, ignoring the twigs and trunks that clutched and scraped her rider.

"Ow!" Dustin exclaimed through clenched teeth. Abruptly, Cricket stopped. They had reached the creek.

"I don't think this is the right spot," Dustin said as he yanked his flashlight from his pocket. He directed its warm beam at the creek. "I guess it's not too steep," he said uncertainly.

He pressed his legs tightly around the horse, but she danced sideways. "Come on, Cricket. It's just a little water. I thought Alice had you better trained than this!"

Cricket's head came up, and she gazed intently across the creek. Voices. Laughter. The thud of horses' hooves on a soft trail. The mare's ears went forward as she whinnied a greeting to her friends approaching through the woods.

"Shut up! You'll give us away!" Dustin leaned forward and tried to clamp his hand over the mare's wide-open mouth. At that moment, she decided to cross the creek.

Before Dustin could get either hand anchored on the saddle horn, Cricket made a tremendous leap, clearing the creek and most of the opposite bank. As she scrambled to the top, Dustin tumbled off. His flashlight somersaulted with him and disappeared into the water.

Dustin grunted as he landed in the slime at the edge of the creek. Then he staggered up, slipped, and fell backwards. His sneakers were flooded, and his blanket drank the cold water thirstily. When he squished out onto the slippery shore, his cape felt ten pounds heavier. Dustin glowered up the embankment at the dark silhouette of his former mount.

"Alice is gonna kill me," he muttered. "Nice Cricket. Don't run away . . . please!" But Cricket was intent on other matters. With a happy nicker she trotted off toward her stablemates.

Tripping over fallen branches as well as his cape, Dustin trailed after her. He wished he were at home watching a movie and gobbling down pizza.

A thick curtain of darkness enveloped him. Where had that mare gone? He could just see the hayride coming through the trees. Shivering, his teeth chattering, he ducked behind a bush.

I'm freezing, Dustin thought dismally. He watched the wagon roll past just beyond his shelter. All plans for terrorizing the hayride were as submerged as his flashlight. By now Cricket was probably halfway home. Dustin imagined the warmth of heaped straw and began trudging after the departing wagon.

"Hey! Wait for me!" he called. His sister's friends were singing and talking. No one answered him. Dustin began to run. He waved his plastic sword and yelled.

Someone on the wagon shined a flashlight toward him, and the light pierced his eyes. One of the girls screamed. A boy shouted. The wagon lurched forward as Peaches and Cream broke into a trot, leaving Dustin farther and farther behind.

His breath was ragged, and he put his hands on his soggy knees and bent over in defeat. Another great adventure gone down the tubes, he thought sadly. Now the only things left were the long walk home and facing Alice when she discovered he'd ridden her precious horse without asking . . . and let her run off in the dark.

Dustin straightened up with a sigh. He turned around and headed back toward home. He could still hear some screams echoing through the woods, and he began to grin. At least he'd managed to scare Alice's silly friends.

Soon the wagon would be coming to the end of the trail. Then Cindy would turn the team around and head back. With each soggy step, Dustin became more determined to stay ahead of the hayride. If he could get home before them, maybe he'd be able to catch Cricket. Maybe Alice wouldn't find out. Maybe the whole adventure could be salvaged.

Speckles of moonlight were strewn along the trail. Dustin followed them, wishing he had his flashlight. The dark woods loomed around and over him. Something made a squeaking noise, causing Dustin to jump and stumble into a bush at the edge of the path.

It was spooky being all alone in the woods. On Cricket's back Dustin hadn't had time to feel scared. Don't be dumb, he told himself. There's nothing here but trees and stuff.

What was that? Nothing. Or was it? Maybe he should wait for the wagon. There it was again! Something was following him, thumping along behind him on the trail. Dustin turned around and saw a large shape approaching. For one second he was frozen with fear.

Then the mare reached out and nuzzled his shoulder with her soft lips. Dustin grabbed the dangling reins and patted Cricket's neck. "Who do you think you are, My Friend Flicka or somethin'?"

He mounted carefully, wrapping the wet cape around his legs so it wouldn't bother the horse. They jogged all the way home, and Dustin did not even notice the faint prickle of that splinter. What was a splinter to a boy who had braved frigid water and a dark woods? He was pleased to arrive back at the barn well ahead of the hayride.

"We make a good pair," Dustin told Cricket as he turned her loose in the paddock. "Maybe next year we'll try some barrel races. Alice is gettin' more interested in boys than horses anyhow."

He returned to the rec room through the same

stairway, only now there were no cobwebs. It seemed he'd been gone a long time, yet the movie was still blaring, and Jessica hadn't disturbed a fold in her covers.

Dustin turned off the VCR. He dumped his wet cape, jeans, sneakers, and socks in the shower stall. Wearing only his underwear, he crawled beneath the blanket and into his sleeping bag. The old dog gave him a sloppy kiss on the cheek. Dustin settled next to her warm, furry back and lay tensely until he heard the hayriders coming into the house.

"There was a maniac out in the woods!"

"He tried to jump in the wagon!"

"It was just some kid dressed up!"

"I bet it was an escaped prisoner!"

A satisfied glow added to the warmth inside Dustin's sleeping bag.

The door to the basement opened, and he heard someone step onto the top landing.

"Dustin?"

"Yeah, Dad?"

"You okay, son?"

Dustin smoothed the blanket and wriggled his chilled toes. "Sure!"

"Just thought I'd check," said his father.

"We're fine, Jessie and me," Dustin said heartily. "How was the hayride?" He tried to sound casual.

"From all accounts, great. You'd think our woods was haunted, to hear them talk. Bet the only one having more fun was the spook."

Dustin got very still. His father cleared his throat and

asked, "You got enough covers down there?"

He nodded, then realized that his father couldn't see him from the top of the stairs. "I'm fine, Dad. No problem."

"That's good." There was a moment of silence; then he added, "When I came down and checked before, looked like Jessica was hogging the covers."

Dustin sat up and stared at the steps. But from this angle, he could only see his father's dusty work shoes.

"We're okay," Dustin said. "Thanks, Dad."

The feet moved up, but there was no sound of the door shutting.

"Uh, Dad?"

"What, Dustin?"

"You're right. The spook did have fun . . . sort of."

"That's good to hear. 'Night, son."

" 'Night, Dad."

The basement door thumped softly shut.

THE STRAYS

As I stepped off the school bus, I heard the horse whinny. He had his head out over the lower half of the stall door, and he was looking right at me when he opened his wide mouth and whinnied like crazy again. I knew he wasn't glad to see me, though. That wasn't why he was screaming.

"Shut up!" I yelled at him. As if he understood, he spun around and disappeared into the stall, leaving a square, empty hole where his head had been. I swallowed hard and kept going up the driveway and around to the back door.

Inside I took one quick sniff, forgetting for a second that there'd be no scent of fresh-baked cookies on this Friday.

"Hi, Brent," Mrs. McCormick said. She was sitting at

the kitchen table with a full cup of tea cradled in her hands. "How'd it go today?"

"Fine." I went to the refrigerator, poured myself a glass of milk, took one sip, and wished I could spit it out. Nothing tasted right today.

When I turned around, Mrs. McCormick was looking out the window toward the stable. "He's been doing that all day," she said softly, as if she were talking to herself. Once again I heard Ember's shrill neigh.

I looked back at the refrigerator door. There was one of my math papers taped up there—a rare A.

"I suppose we should have let him see Sky's body. Maybe that would have helped," Mrs. McCormick said slowly.

Why couldn't she just shut up? I wondered. Her mentioning the other horse's name made me feel strange. Just yesterday Sky had slipped on a patch of ice in the pasture. We found him lying there, and she asked me to run to the house and call the vet. I was sure he'd be okay. I thought that stuff about killing horses with broken legs was all ancient history.

But when the vet came, he didn't help. I only half heard snatches of talk—something about Sky's being so old—at least twenty-seven . . . bones wouldn't mend . . . the best thing to do. . . . And then they told me to take Ember back to his stall. I stayed in there with him, and after a while I heard the vet's truck pull away and then Mrs. McCormick sort of snuffling as she went past the stable and into the house.

I just sat there on a bale of hay, watching Ember eat

his oats. When he finished, he looked over at the next stall and twisted his head around, searching. Then he whinnied. That's when I left.

Later on a truck came and took Sky's body, but I never saw it. And neither did Ember.

Last night I heard Ember calling off and on. I had trouble sleeping. I had a pain in my belly, like something was gnawing away at my insides. I was cold, too, even after I got up and added an extra blanket to my bed. But I'm used to it. Ever since I was six years old and my mom left me at her friend Tonya's house and didn't come back, I've had stomachaches and chills. The only way to deal with that awful feeling is to make myself numb.

Don't feel. Don't talk. And most of all, don't cry. People make fun of you when you cry. When you're a foster kid, it's important to be tough.

Now Mrs. McCormick was talking about Sky's body, and I could sense a pain starting down inside me, where nobody could reach. I stood real still for a second and stared at the grocery list stuck to the refrigerator by a magnet in the shape of a frog. I made my mind sort of blank and numb, just looking at the silly frog.

Then I heard Mrs. McCormick sigh. Funny, I thought, how somebody could get so attached to a horse. Out of the corner of my eye, I saw her pick up her cup, take it to the sink, and dump out the cold tea.

I wasn't exactly prepared for what she did next. She took a step toward me and put one arm around my shoulder. I got real stiff. I don't like people touching me, even when they're being nice. But I didn't say anything or even move away.

"Brent?" Mrs. McCormick said softly. She waited a second, and when I didn't answer, she let her arm slip off me and stepped back a little so she could look at my face.

"I've been so sad today, but I got a phone call this afternoon that took my mind off Sky's death." She hesitated, but I didn't ask any questions or show any curiosity. She continued, talking kind of quickly now. "The call was from Mrs. Woods. She had some news for you . . . and us."

I still wasn't looking at Mrs. McCormick, and when I just stood there, not saying a word, even when she mentioned the name of my social worker, I guess she gave up trying to reach me. She went back to the sink and started rinsing her cup and spoon.

I was about to head for my bedroom when Mrs. McCormick said something that made me freeze.

"Mrs. Woods has talked to your birth mom again."

I tried to make my heart stop doing weird stuff.

"Your birth mother has signed all the necessary papers, and she wants the agency to make an adoption plan for you. I guess things just aren't coming together for her, and she feels you need a permanent home now that you're a teenager."

Mrs. McCormick's voice seemed to be coming from far away, and there was a strange humming noise in my ears.

"You okay, Brent?" she asked.

I took another step toward the doorway and nodded.

"I wanted to tell you right away, Brent. Dan and I would love to adopt you and have you be our son. It would mean so much to us. We really like you and would be proud to be your parents."

What did she expect? Did she think I'd jump up and down and yell "Goody, goody! Now I have a real mommy!"?

But maybe she didn't expect anything, because she just kept on talking.

"You know, Brent, at your age, the social workers will be consulting you, too. If you decide not to stay with us, the agency will start looking for another home for you."

Another home? Fine with me, I thought. That's what I'm used to—moving around like a stray dog. But all I said was "I'll think about it." Then I retreated to my room.

I lay down on the bed and forced the numbness to take over. I turned up my radio as loud as I knew Mrs. McCormick would stand. I'd lived here for half a year and pretty much knew what was okay and what wasn't. After being with seven different foster families, I was good at figuring people out.

But now I wasn't so sure about the McCormicks. I had never had *anyone* tell me that they wanted me to be their son. Not even my own mother wanted me. Maybe that wasn't fair. Maybe she really did want me, but she just couldn't handle being a parent. But it all came down to the same thing: me not being able to live with her. I gulped and punched my pillow as hard as I could.

My thoughts were as tangled as wet, knotted shoelaces. Did the McCormicks really want me? Or was Mrs. McCormick so sure that I'd decide to leave that she felt safe saying they wanted me? I didn't want to think about anything. I shut my eyes.

I woke up with a jerk. How long had I slept? I heard people talking in the kitchen just down the hallway. I recognized Mr. McCormick's voice and guessed it must be almost time for supper.

Then I heard Mrs. McCormick say "I wish you wouldn't let him out."

For just a second, I thought she was talking about me, and I sat up.

"Dear, the ice has all melted," said her husband. "Besides, Ember is lots younger and more surefooted than Sky ever was. He's not going to fall on anything. And he's going crazy in that stall. He's got a path beaten down from pacing round and round."

"I know. He's been crying all day."

"I guess you're right. That's what he's doing—crying for Sky. But he just misses him. He doesn't understand," Mr. McCormick said.

"Well, I know just how he feels," she said sadly.

Supper that night was almost normal. Ember must have wandered off to the far edge of the pasture, because we couldn't hear him calling unless we all got really quiet and listened. So the two of them talked a lot. I even tried to cheer them up by telling some of the stupid stuff that had happened at school.

The only time horses were mentioned was when we were clearing the table and Mr. McCormick said, "Maybe we'll buy another horse for you to ride, Brent."

I didn't answer, and Mrs. McCormick said, "It all depends. . . ." She left her words dangling. I wondered if she was thinking, The kid will be leaving anyway, so why bother?

Later in bed, I couldn't help listening for Ember, but all I could hear was the sorry-sounding wind. Probably because of that nap I'd taken, I was wide awake. My mind kept going back to all the other places I'd lived. I'd never stayed with people who had horses before, only ones with dogs or cats—and once with a lady who had 14 canaries. She used a lot of old newspaper.

When I first came here, I was afraid of horses. But a foster kid has to act brave, so I learned to keep my fear under control. Mr. McCormick taught me to ride. I always rode Sky because, according to the McCormicks, he was the older, more reliable of the two horses. But he had some tricks he tried to pull on me.

Sky never liked to leave the place by himself, and when I'd get him to the end of the driveway, he'd do a little dance while I tried to keep him going. And whenever he wanted me to loosen the reins, he'd just take that big old head of his and stick it way out, and the reins would slip through my fingers before I knew what was happening. Then he'd have lots of room to maybe take a grab for some grass.

I learned real fast that you couldn't tie Sky to a tree or a post or anything. He knew how to untie almost any knot. He'd work at it with his teeth and toss his head up and down until it'd come loose. A real tough knot he'd get around by slipping off the whole halter. He'd rub his ears against the post and catch the top of the halter or bridle, and after a while it would slide off, just like that. He wouldn't run off or anything. I'd find him about three feet from the place he'd been tied, eating grass. He'd look up at me as if to say "Now why'd you tie me in the first place? I had no plans on leaving."

The part I liked best about Sky was the way he'd ask me for a treat. He'd just sort of nuzzle me softly with those big lips, fumbling at my pockets or fingers. But he'd never bite me.

Now I rolled over and curled myself into a little ball under the covers. Shut up! I told my brain. But it took a long time for the safe numbness to return.

In the morning it was always my job to feed the dog and the three cats who lived around the stable. Then I'd help Mr. McCormick with the horses. I had to check the water trough to make sure it was full, and next I'd climb into the loft and drag a bale of hay to the hole in the floor and yell "Bombs away!" before dropping it down.

This morning, being Saturday, I got up a little later than usual. But the sky was dull gray, like somebody had put a lid over the earth. Mr. McCormick was still getting dressed, so I went out alone. I walked to the outside trough, petting the dog, Oscar, who was leaping up and down at my side. The heater in the trough was turned on, so there was no ice.

I glanced around, looking for Ember. Usually, he would've been right there with Sky, checking me out, begging for his oats.

I whistled and listened. Nothing. That's when I noticed the gate. It was open. Now how'd that happen? I wondered. Then I realized what an open gate must mean. I looked around the yard and didn't see any sign of the horse.

"Brent?" Mr. McCormick called from the doorway of the house. "Is Ember okay? We just got the strangest phone call. Somebody asking if we were missing a horse."

"The gate's open," I called back. "The latch is broken."

We started our search at Mrs. Kendle's. She was the lady who had called. She told us that her oldest son kept insisting that he'd heard a horse trot past their house very early in the morning. Since he was only five and had a vivid imagination, at first she ignored him. But when he kept talking about it, she finally decided to call us. The kid's name was Nick, and he was real shy and quiet. But he came outside on their front porch and pointed in the direction he'd heard the horse go.

We drove down the road and stopped at the next farm, but those people hadn't seen or heard anything. So we continued on, stopping at each place we came to. Some people gave us a funny look when we asked about a stray horse, but a surprising number said that yes, as a matter of fact, they had heard hoofbeats.

Five miles we drove, right into Fragglesville, where the old guy at the general store said, "Yup. Bob Mitchell was in and said he had a lost horse in his farmyard."

We found Ember standing in muck with about twenty Holstein heifers eyeing him. I put on his halter and led him out, carefully shutting and latching the gate behind me. Mr. McCormick went up to the house to thank Bob Mitchell while Ember and I started along the road. We hadn't brought his bridle, and I wouldn't have wanted to ride him anyhow. Sky had been my horse.

I kept Ember off to the side of the road in the dried-up grass, and in about five minutes, Mr. McCormick caught up with us and drove alongside.

"How you doing, Brent?" he asked.

"Okay."

"Think you can make it back on your own? I could go on ahead and get that gate fixed."

"Sure, we're fine."

"Well, all right. Take it easy. No rush."

I nodded in agreement.

Mr. McCormick smiled at me, and I looked away fast. Sometimes smiles can be a lot like touching. They make me uncomfortable.

"See you later, son," he said. Then he accelerated slowly and left Ember and me alone.

He was gone, but his words were suspended in the air around me. "See you later, son." Son! My eyes were filling up—from the cold, I tried to tell myself.

I sniffed. I wanted Sky back. I wanted my mom back. I wanted the safe numbness to return, but it wouldn't.

Suddenly I stopped and just stood there, shivering and blowing on my cold fingers. Then I reached up and straightened Ember's messy forelock. He pushed his nose toward me, and all of a sudden I was hugging him around the neck and crying like crazy.

I wiped my face with the sleeve of my jacket. It was cold, but inside, somewhere really deep down, I felt warm.

This was going to be a long walk, but I didn't mind. I would use the time to decide how to tell the McCormicks that they should buy another horse. Maybe two. That way all three of us could go riding—like a real family.

"No more being a stray," I said to Ember. I think he understood that I was talking about both of us.

A Horse for all Seasons

– WINTER –

WISH UPON A STAR

In the doorway Lynda paused. Above the rhythmic creak of a floorboard, she could hear her eight-year-old sister's high-pitched, excited whisper.

". . . first star I see tonight. I wish I may, I wish I might, have the wish I wish tonight."

Holding her breath, Lynda peered around the door-jamb. Becca was sitting in her special rocking chair, facing the window.

"I wish I'd get a horse for Christmas."

Lynda let her breath escape with a sigh. Frowning slightly, she marched into their bedroom and slung her books on her bed. The cat, Cinder, got up indignantly and moved to the floor.

"You-you wished the s-same thing last night, Becca," Lynda said.

"Stop listening, then." Becca turned her whole body toward her sister.

Lynda shrugged. She couldn't say anything more, not while looking at Becca.

The little girl's eyes were lost in the smudged hollows of her pale face. Her hair was pressed flat in some spots and sticking up in others from wearing her hat home from school. Leaning over stiffly, she grabbed her crutches.

Lynda watched Becca struggle to her feet but knew better than to offer to help. Instead she plopped onto her bed and began riffling through her math book to find her assignment.

"Look at Prince," Becca said as she held up a black model horse. "He's lost one of his mares, and he's going to go looking for her."

"F-fine. Just be quiet." Lynda bent over her book.

The assignment was addition and subtraction of fractions—easy stuff that she remembered from last year. Besides, she liked fractions. The numbers never got too big. Long division was discouraging, with all those huge numbers that wandered all over the page. Carefully she began to copy the first problem on her notebook paper. Suddenly the silence was pierced by a shrill whinny.

"B-Becca! I told you to be q-quiet!"

Becca grinned. "It wasn't me. It was Prince. He's calling his mare."

Lynda shook her head in mock disgust. She let her gaze drift around their cluttered bedroom. Every wall was decorated with horse pictures from the calendars that their parents gave them each Christmas. Whenever one of the pictures fell down, Lynda had to go find some tape and stick it back up.

Becca had names for all the horses. Over there, taped up next to the window, was one they called Flash. He was black with a white blaze, and he was standing in snow, looking right out at them. And above Becca's bed was a picture of a mare, her golden mane and tail lifted by a silent wind. Beside her was a perky foal. They were grazing in a lush pasture. The mare was named Sunshine. Lynda and Becca had argued about the foal's name because Becca insisted it was a filly, and Lynda said it looked like a colt. But finally she had let her sister have her way, although she thought Sally was a ridiculous name for a horse, even a little girl horse.

Sometimes Lynda did that—just gave in to Becca. There were so many things Becca couldn't do. She had had rheumatoid arthritis ever since she was three. Just getting up in the morning was a problem. Whenever kids at school asked Lynda "What's the matter with your sister?" she always told them, but usually they didn't believe her. They thought arthritis was something just old people got.

"*My* horse is going to be just like Prince," Becca said with complete confidence.

"I-I suppose," said Lynda, "that S-Santa's going to bring him down the furnace pipe, and you're going to put him in our teeny yard. Do-do you think S-Santa would really give a city kid a horse?"

Becca frowned. "Maybe I could keep him at the riding stable in Sunset Park." She glanced toward the window that overlooked the park.

"N-no way." Lynda shook her head. "That's just for horses the park district owns. Be-besides, we'd never have enough money for a horse. And I read in the paper that the city isn't sure it can afford to keep the stable open. If it can't pay for horses, how could we?"

"They've got dozens. I just want one!" was Becca's stubborn reply.

Lynda bit her lip thoughtfully. She knew Becca couldn't ride a horse anyhow. Not with her legs hurting so much.

If wishes did come true, Lynda thought, I'd wish I didn't stutter and Becca could walk right and ride a horse. She looked out their window at the trees, an intricate lacing of bare branches and twigs. The sky was the same dense gray as Cinder's fur. She couldn't see a single star.

"Hey, B-Becca! How'd you see a star? It's cloudy and starting to snow again. I-I bet you wished on some dumb airplane light."

"I did not!" Becca squealed. She hated to make a mistake. "See? There it is. Just above the biggest maple tree."

"I-I guess you're right. N-no, wait! I think that's Venus. Venus isn't a star. It's a planet."

"So what? But just to make you happy, I'll do it over. Planet light, Planet bright. . . ." Becca modified the chant, ending with "I still wish I could have a horse!"

"O-okay, okay," Lynda said gently. She couldn't help admiring her sister's persistence. "N-now I have to do my homework, so be quiet."

After Becca went to sleep that night, Lynda lay awake. Cinder pounced onto the bed and kneaded his way toward her face. She petted him, hard and firm, trying to press him against the blankets so he'd go to sleep.

She stared at him. Silhouetted against the soft glow from the streetlight outside, he looked large, sort of like a panther. Lynda had seen one last summer at the zoo. A zoo, she thought, is like a stable for wild animals. Her thoughts seemed to be stumbling around in the dark. Becca . . . horses . . . stables . . . Becca . . . panthers . . . zoos. . . . And then, quite suddenly, Lynda remembered a zoo advertisement she'd read in a magazine, and she sat up so quickly, Cinder bounced right off the bed.

The next morning on the way to school, Lynda stopped at the corner mailbox, then looked back toward her house. She could see her footprints in the new snow, weaving in and out among other people's. But none of the tracks belonged to Becca, who was at home struggling into her coat, getting ready for her special bus.

Lynda unslung her backpack and carefully slipped an envelope out of the outermost pocket. For a moment she stared at it. Her idea didn't seem quite so clever in the glare of sun and snow. But she took a quick breath and dropped the letter into the mailbox. With a clang, the metal trapdoor sprang shut. Done! She couldn't get it back now.

For the next two weeks Lynda's heart skipped every time she heard the phone ring. But it was never for her. Each day when she got home she checked the mail for a letter. But there was never one with her name on it.

By the time the day before Christmas arrived, Lynda was feeling as sullen and grumpy as the weather. For two days the sun had sulked behind a murky wall of clouds and the temperature had been hanging around 33 degrees. The top layer of snow had turned the color of old oatmeal, and the sidewalks were covered with slush.

Early in the afternoon, the temperature dropped, and it began to snow. Becca asked to have her rocker brought down from her room so she could sit near both the living room window and the Christmas tree.

"We're going to have a white Christmas!" she told everyone at least ten times, until Lynda wanted to clap her hands over her ears—or over Becca's mouth.

After supper, Becca dragged out their well-worn copy of *How the Grinch Stole Christmas!* and insisted on reading it aloud to anyone who'd listen. She had just come to the part where little Cindy-Lou Who asks the Grinch why he's taking their Christmas tree, "Why?"

Lynda was searching all over their own Christmas tree, trying to find the little drummer boy ornament, her favorite.

"W-where'd you put it, Mom?" she asked.

"Oh, somewhere. I can't remember. Or maybe it got broken last year. Didn't it?"

"No, it didn't!" Lynda said vehemently, although she wasn't sure.

"Maybe Cinder knocked it on the floor," suggested their father.

"Hey!" said Becca indignantly. "I'm reading."

"Well, th-that's a stupid story, anyhow," said Lynda as she peered under the tree. "Everything turns out p-perfect in the end, b-but nothing's really perfect. Even on Christmas Eve."

"Shut up!" yelled Becca.

"Girls, please!" said their mother.

Lynda was just about to yell back at Becca when she saw the drummer boy ornament hanging nearly hidden by the trunk of the tree. His tiny arms were raised, the tips of his drumsticks just about to strike his drum.

Tap. Tap. Tap.

Someone was knocking at the front door.

Dad went through the enclosed porch, and Lynda could hear voices. Probably some neighbor, she thought, bringing a nasty-tasting fruitcake. She didn't feel any better for having found her favorite ornament. She wished she were little again and believed in Santa or even the Grinch.

"They're here!" Dad called. "Girls, time to bundle up. There's a little Christmas present outside!"

"Really? Great!" exclaimed Mom, hopping up and rushing to get Becca's snowsuit. "Lynda, hurry! Get your coat on, and don't forget a hat and scarf and mittens. And here, honey, read this." She pulled a creased letter out of her pocket and shoved it into Lynda's hand.

Lynda's eyes skimmed the letter. It was to her parents from a lady who worked at the city's riding stable.

"Your daughter, Lynda," the letter began, "has written to us and given us a fantastic idea for raising money to keep our stable open. She has suggested we have a 'sponsor a horse' program similar to the idea used to support the animals at many zoos."

The best part was later, near the end of the letter: ". . . and we have the perfect horse for Lynda's little sister . . . will try to bring him to give your girls a sleigh ride . . ." There was more, but everyone was leaving the house now, and Lynda had to grab her coat. She dashed after her mother, jamming her hands into her mittens as she crossed the snowy street. Dad was carrying Becca.

"Mom! W-wait!" Lynda caught her mother's arm and spoke demandingly into her ear. "How come you didn't tell me?"

"Oh, Lynda, I'm sorry," Mom whispered back. "I guess I just wanted to make sure it would really happen before I told you. I didn't want you to get your hopes up and then have nothing work out. And look, the weather's perfect and everything! If it hadn't snowed, they couldn't have come."

"So, do you like him, Becca?" Dad asked as they all gathered around the brightly painted sleigh, the small dark horse, and the young woman holding him. She had a park district emblem on her coat.

"Oh, yeah!" Becca's voice was filled with awe. "Where'd he come from?"

"Well, I guess the North Pole," said the woman, grinning broadly, "by way of Sunset Stables. Santa told me to bring him right here. This is 130 Gramercy Road, right?"

Becca nodded her head slightly.

"Well, here he is. And Santa says that since your parents are going to be helping to pay for his food, he belongs to you."

"Me?" asked Becca with a little squeal.

"Yup, he's yours! Unless, of course, your sister wants you to share him."

"N-no, that's okay," Lynda said quickly. "Becca's the one who wants a horse. I've got a cat already."

"Good! Of course, this horse can't live in your house. We'll keep him for you at the stables, but you can come and visit him anytime you want," the park lady said.

"Merry Christmas, Becca," said Lynda.

Mom reached over, squeezed Lynda's arm, and whispered, "Thanks, Santa."

Lynda shook her head and whispered back, "You're th-thanking the Grinch." She did feel as if her heart suddenly had grown three sizes bigger.

Dad lifted Becca into the sleigh and waited for Lynda to climb in beside her before tucking the blanket around their legs. After the park lady settled on the seat, she clucked to the horse, and he started forward, the bells on his harness jingling like the sound of children's distant laughter. The light from the sleigh's lantern opened a golden path through the darkness in front of them.

The horse began to trot, and the sleigh rushed forward, skimming effortlessly over the snowy trails. On both sides dark tree trunks passed in a blur.

It was as if they were on a magical ship, sailing through the night. The horse's long tail swept back, and snowflakes danced in its wake. Lynda drank in the sparkling cold air.

She wanted the ride to go on forever, but too soon they were back in front of their house, and their parents were there to help them out of the sleigh.

"Let me pet him! Please, Daddy," said Becca. Her father carried her to the horse's head.

"Oh, Daddy, it's wonderful! My wish came true. Isn't he beautiful? What's his name? I forgot to ask. Oh, no. Don't tell us. Let us guess. You first, Daddy."

"Is it Black Beauty?"

The park lady shook her head.

"I bet it's Prancer, like one of Santa's reindeer," said Mom.

"Wrong again. Sorry."

"Your turn, Lynda," Becca said.

Lynda squinted at the handsome horse. "Is-is it Prince?"

" 'Fraid not."

Becca was nearly falling from her father's arms in her excitement. "My turn. I know his name. It's Star!"

"Right! How'd you guess?" asked the young woman.

"I didn't *guess*," said Becca. "I knew his name was Star. I just knew."

Lynda ran her mitten-webbed fingers beneath the horse's mane. He turned his head and looked at her with deep, gentle eyes. "Wishing Star," Lynda whispered so only the horse could hear her. Holding out her hand, she felt his warm breath right through her mitten.

FROSTED FIRE

Over and over her father had told her "He's not the same horse. He's changed." But Sara had refused to believe him.

Now she stomped her feet hard on the gravel floor, trying to jar some feeling back into her half-frozen toes. She reached up and gently stroked the tall gray gelding's neck.

"Do you think Dad's right?" asked her younger brother, Jay.

Sara shrugged, then swung into the saddle and turned Frosty toward the open space in the center of the machine shed. Riding inside was depressing, with the dim, dull light and the hulking tractors watching sullenly from either side. But the fields and ring were snow-covered, and she had to keep working with her horse every day if she was ever going to prove that her father was wrong.

"Easy, honey," she whispered to Frosty as she rubbed beneath his dark mane. But she felt no relaxation in the horse's tense body.

Focusing her gaze on the low jump at the far end of the shed, she tried to suppress her misgivings. Carefully, lightly, she pressed her legs against Frosty's sides, urging him into a trot. He sprang forward too fast and became unbalanced, unsteady.

The air on her face felt cold as she turned him in a tight circle. She'd been working with him for weeks, going over all the basics, yet he didn't feel ready.

As they cantered toward the low hurdle, it seemed to grow into a solid and forbidding wall. A clutch of fear grasped Sara's throat. Abruptly, she turned Frosty to one side and pulled him to a halt.

"He won't do it, will he?" Jay said.

Sara shook her head. "I don't know. I decided not to try it."

With Jay trailing behind, she led Frosty back to the stables. Maybe he wouldn't jump anymore, but at least he belonged to her now. Officially. She'd always thought of Frosty as her horse, even though he'd been foaled at her uncle's horse farm. She had been the one to ride him for two unforgettable years, winning in one show after another. When Uncle Matt was offered an incredibly high price for his young champion, he couldn't resist. After all, as he pointed out to Sara, that was his business—raising and training and *selling* horses.

Unfortunately for Frosty, he'd been bought by the parents of a young girl with inadequate riding experience. When she'd tried to jump him, she'd fallen off, hanging on to the reins, and given the horse's tender mouth a vicious yank. On another ride she fell again. Only this time she broke her arm, and the horse was blamed.

A dismal succession of owners followed, none able to control the now-skittish horse, until finally one contacted Uncle Matt to complain. Sara's parents offered to buy Frosty. He was no longer a good jumper, and they could afford the price. Frosty had come home a few weeks before Christmas, thin and frightened, but finally hers.

Now Sara put one cold-stiffened hand into her pocket. Amid the tissues, bits of string, and candy wrappers, her numb fingers located a lump of sugar. When she offered it on her palm, Frosty took it with gentle lips. But when she reached to pet him, he drew back; the memory of rough treatment was too strong.

That night Sara flopped on her rumpled bed, exhausted and discouraged. She knew she'd need to get up early to feed Frosty before school, so she set her alarm clock before turning off her light.

When a screaming noise woke her, she reached for her clock and pushed the button, but the wail went on and on.

An alarm. A smoke alarm!

Instinctively, she rolled out of bed and hit the floor with a dull thump.

Get out! ordered a tiny voice inside her head. Sara groped toward the window and touched its cold, hard surface. *Open it!* said the voice. In the tarry blackness, she could smell smoke—even taste it.

The window was stuck, and Sara's hands were growing weak. *It's too late.*

Suddenly a powerful draft of winter-cold air burst in her face. The window was open! She could hear her father's strong, sure voice, clearing away the fog that had been clouding her mind.

"Sara! Climb out!"

With trembling knees, she followed him down the ladder. Outside on the snowy ground, Sara hugged Jay and her mom.

"We've got to call the fire department!" her father said, then gave a hard, wheezing cough.

"Hank, no! You can't go back inside." Her mother grabbed hold of his pajama shirt tail. "I'll go call from the Bancrofts'. Oh, no, the car keys are in my purse—inside!"

They all stared silently at the house. The moon was shining; there was almost no wind.

Sara thought the scene looked like a Christmas card depicting a peaceful house at midnight with a full moon, but without Santa's tiny reindeer arched above the rooftop. But instead of the tinkling of sleigh bells, she could hear the smoke alarm, its pulsating scream muted by walls and distance. Smoke was coming from their escape windows in sinister, shimmering puffs.

"I'll go," said Jay, turning to run up the long driveway.

"No!" Sara's cry stopped him. "I will. On Frosty. I can cut across the fields."

As she ran toward the barn, Jay followed. "Here, take my coat," he offered, shedding it as he caught up with her at Frosty's stall door.

"Thanks." Sara put it on. After she led Frosty out, Jay gave her a leg up.

"Go for it," he said tensely.

With a quick nod, Sara urged Frosty forward. Across the wide pasture they galloped, plowing through drifts that would have trapped a person on foot. The tears in her eyes felt like bits of ice.

Somewhere up ahead was the rail fence that separated their property from the Bancrofts'. A fence with a gate. But where was it?

Then she saw a dark set of lines etched into the snow. She realized that Frosty saw the fence, too, for his stride altered just slightly. Find the gate, she told herself. That's the sensible thing to do.

Yes! There it was. She jumped off before Frosty had completely stopped.

Fumbling with the icy latch . . . fingers stumbling. Finally! It was undone. But when she tried to swing the gate open, it wouldn't budge. One side was frozen to the ground beneath a snowdrift. A sob caught in her throat as she sagged, defeated, against the rails.

But inside Sara's mind the fire was creeping and crackling, destroying her home. She had to do something! Using the gate, she remounted and trotted Frosty away, then turned him to face the fence.

Her tears made the dark lines of the fence blur as if they were melting. Suddenly her fear of the jump was gone. Her fear. Frosty's fear. It was all mixed together. She understood that now.

Sara could feel the horse gathering himself beneath her, and then he plunged into a canter. She looked beyond the fence, thought beyond it.

It was a smooth, high jump, with no hesitation, no mistake. They swept across the field and up Bancrofts' lane.

"Fire! Fire!" Sara screamed, riding right up to the porch steps. For a long, dreadful moment the house seemed dead and empty, but then the porch light flooded on, the door swung wide, and there was Mrs. Bancroft.

She ran down the steps and helped Sara off her horse. "Call the fire department!" she yelled to her husband as he came to the door.

Later, Sara was standing next to her family and the Bancrofts, who had brought her home. The fire fighters were tramping about, their hoses stretching like giant deflated snakes on the snow.

"Smoke damage," said Mr. Bancroft. "Bad, but sure could've been a lot worse. We're just glad you all got out safely."

Sara's father nodded. "The firemen tell me that if they hadn't gotten here when they did, the whole place would've gone up in flames."

"You can thank Sara," said Mrs. Bancroft, "and her horse. Isn't that the same horse she rode in all those shows?"

Sara looked at her father. In the pale light that was beginning to seep across the eastern sky, she saw him nod as he said, "Yes, he's the same horse."

HEARTS AND HOOFBEATS

The first time I saw Colin, he was walking on top of a fence. At Mason's Stables most of the fences are made of wood, but this section was heavy-gauge barbed wire.

Whoever built it did a good job, because it was strong enough to hold Colin. He was taking careful steps, placing his feet sideways between the jagged barbs. Like a tightrope walker, he held his arms straight out from his narrow body.

I had just come from around the corner of the smaller barn, and he didn't notice me. Otherwise, I'd have thought he was showing off. Some boys are like that, punching each other or burping to make an impression, but not ever wondering what *sort* of impression they're making. There are lots of jerks like that in my eighth grade class at Washington Junior High. But this kid was different.

So I stopped and watched. I was on my way to check on my bay gelding. His name is Surprise because he was a surprise present from my dad after he moved out and my parents got divorced.

Before my dad left, the only thing I'd wanted was a horse of my own. After he was gone, all I wanted was for Dad to come home.

He didn't. I got Surprise instead. I guess Dad thought that would make up for everything: all those years of listening to my parents' arguments, and finally them getting split up for keeps. My horse was a bribe. Shut up, kid. Stop complaining. A horse—like a cookie or a lollipop. But I hadn't let it work.

Although I came to Mason's Stables to check on Surprise every few days after school, I didn't ride him. And whenever Dad asked "How's your horse?" I'd just shrug or say "Oh, he's okay, I guess." I wanted Dad to think that I didn't care.

That's why I was there that September afternoon watching a strange kid sway on an ugly stretch of fence, my breath caught between my teeth.

Three steps. That's all he managed. Then he lost his balance and sprang off and landed directly in front of me. Safe. He didn't act embarrassed. He just bowed like somebody in a play, and glanced at me with gray, pale eyes that looked wrong with his mop of dark hair.

"You're Maria," he said as his gaze wandered away to the horses in the field.

I nodded.

He had the build of an acrobat, small and neat, with muscles that made me think he was older than his height suggested.

"You own the bay Arabian gelding." He spoke in a quick, firm voice that went well with his body.

"Surprise?" I asked stupidly. There was something about this kid that confused me. I didn't wonder where he came from. Not then. I just accepted his jumping right into my messed-up life.

"Yeah, Surprise. You don't ride him."

"No." I could feel a prickle of annoyance at the implied accusation. It reminded me of my mom when she said, "Maria, you can stop moping around now. Half the kids at your school have divorced parents. I thought after your dad gave you that horse, you'd be the happiest girl alive. But you don't even ride him."

"Why not?" Colin asked.

"Because I just don't."

He looked at me. When his pale eyes darted from the horses and fixed on my face, I knew he was seeing me better than anyone had in a long time.

"Then I'll ride him." He turned and headed toward the barn where Surprise was stabled.

"Hey, wait a minute!" I dashed after him. "Who are you? You can't just ride my horse without my say-so."

"I'm Colin. May I ride your horse?"

With an exasperated shrug I answered, "Sure. Why not?"

Surprise gave an expectant nicker when he saw me, but as usual I didn't let his greeting soften my attitude toward him and what he represented.

Colin walked right into that stall like he lived there himself. He started talking real low, addressing the horse, but I had a feeling he wanted me to hear, too.

"She doesn't ride you, huh? Guess she's chicken. Big thing like you. Wild, too, I bet."

"No, he's not," I blurted out. "At least my dad *says* he's well trained. Not that I believe him."

Colin moved all around Surprise, stroking his back, running his fingers down his legs. He even cupped one hand under the horse's chin and looked into his mouth. I stepped back and shoved my hands in my pockets uneasily. "What're you doing?"

He turned and looked at me gravely. "Just checking him over. So, you like Petunia better than this one?"

"Petunia?" I asked. She's the old palomino mare that I'd been taking lessons on before I got Surprise. "She's nice," I said. "But I can't ride her now, 'cause I've got my own horse. That's one thing my parents agree on. They don't think I need lessons anymore."

"Do you?" he asked, slipping my horse's halter on with one easy, confident motion.

"Huh?"

The boy shook his head slowly, as if to clear away my stupidity. "Do you think you need more lessons?" He led Surprise out of the stall, and I jumped out of the way.

"Yeah, I do. I'm no good. I mean, these people here are all great, and I'd feel like a fool riding in front of them on a horse like Surprise. But it's so expensive. We can't afford lessons and the board payments, too. You know. . . ."

My voice trailed off as I realized I was saying things to this kid that I wouldn't have told anyone else. I clamped my mouth shut and vowed to myself to keep quiet.

But Colin didn't make any comments. He just tied Surprise's lead rope in a grooming area and picked up one of his front hooves to examine. I wriggled my toes inside my sneakers and chewed my lower lip.

"Go get his grooming kit, okay?" he asked me.

I trotted off to the tack room at the far end of the barn, glad to escape, if only for a minute. By the time I returned, Colin had finished cleaning out all of Surprise's hooves. He wiped the hoof pick on his dirty jeans and stuck it in his back pocket.

"You do that every day?" he asked, pointing to my horse's feet. He knew I didn't. I'd never done it.

"Who do you think you are, my mother?" I slammed the container of brushes, combs, and polish on the concrete floor. Surprise flung his head back and gave me a startled look.

But Colin just stroked the horse's neck soothingly and said, "It needs to be done. There's a chance of him getting thrush if he stands around with dirty feet."

I didn't answer. For the next hour I did plenty of not answering.

Colin knew a lot about horses, both on and off their backs. While I was watching him canter Surprise around the outdoor arena that first day, my former riding instructor, Sherri, came over and propped her elbows on the rail beside me.

"He's very good," she said.

I nodded. "His name's Colin."

"Yeah, I know. Colin Mason, the owner's son. Smart idea to let him ride your horse, Maria. Maybe you can work out some sort of discount on the boarding fees."

Over the next weeks and months I never got around to asking for a discount. At first I was uncomfortable finding Colin always there when I'd arrive to check on Surprise. I realized that some of the older girls at the stables would have been flattered to be in my position. I could tell by the sidelong glances they'd make as Colin walked by and the way they'd toss their hair and talk a little too loud and giggly.

But I didn't care what they thought. Not one way or the other. And I just put up with Colin because I didn't know what else to do.

"You've got one of the best horses in the stable," Colin told me one day.

I pulled the mane comb gently through Surprise's black forelock. "Could be."

"He's young. Needs to be ridden so he won't forget his training."

I didn't answer, but I started coming every day after school. I'd help Colin groom Surprise and tack him up with the English saddle and bridle. Colin was always dressed in faded jeans and a T-shirt. He'd change his sneakers for scuffed riding boots before mounting. Then he'd be off, working my horse in the outdoor ring until the sweat gleamed on Surprise's smooth neck.

Walk, trot, canter, stand, back—while Colin talked to

Surprise in a low, gentle tone, or sometimes called out to me.

"Watch this, Maria. He's good! Here's a flying lead change."

I'd learned about leads but was still confused. I shivered while Colin and Surprise demonstrated. It was late October by now, and most of the other riders were using the indoor arena. Not Colin. His only concession to the chill was a ragged flannel shirt half-buttoned over his T-shirt.

One day he trotted Surprise over to my perch on the rail fence.

"Your turn," he said simply.

My stomach flopped over. I'm not ready! was what I meant to say. What came out as I slid off the fence was an inaudible moan.

"You know the basics, and so does he," said Colin.

"I haven't ridden in months," I muttered lamely.

Colin grinned. "I know, Maria. But that's all going to change today."

So I rode, but not very well. At first I felt like a foolish scarecrow, flapping around on Surprise's back. I was glad only Colin was watching.

"Relax your back a little," he called. "Now turn your head before the corners and look where you're going. . . . Heels down. . . . Steady your hands. . . . Good . . . very good!"

By the time I dismounted, my knees were trembling, but I'd fallen in love with my horse. I leaned against his neck and breathed in that special, warm, horsey scent.

"Not so bad, was it?" said Colin.

I looked into his pale eyes and knew he already understood. From then on my feelings toward Colin were different, too.

All through November and December we continued to work outside. Colin's father bought a three-year-old filly named Gem, and Colin began schooling her while I rode Surprise.

The weather held, flat and cold and still. The gray sky descended and seemed to become part of the landscape. As we circled the ring, our horses' breath puffed before us, visible for an instant and then gone in the crisp air.

Our conversations usually were about the horses or the dogs and cats who added to the stable population. But one afternoon Colin said, "I hear your parents are divorced."

"Yeah."

"Mine, too," he said.

"Yeah, I've heard." Sherri and a couple of the other kids had given me a few facts about Colin.

"How's it going for you?" he asked.

I shrugged without looking at him. I shied away from talking about my problems the way Gem leaped away from a loud noise. My home life had nothing to do with my time at the stables with Colin and Surprise. I had begun to think we had something special here.

Colin didn't push me to answer, but gradually he told me about himself and his parents. Their divorce three years before had been stormy.

"Some days I felt like I was being squeezed by the pressure," he said. "Other times I was being pulled apart like a rag between two vicious dogs. I tried to keep them together. Even did stupid stuff to try to punish them. I don't think they even noticed. I was just punishing myself."

His mother had won the custody battle, and Colin had moved with her to Maryland.

"She's a veterinarian specializing in horses. I go out with her to these fancy stables, and I'm learning a lot. I've been riding for one guy, showing some of his jumpers the past two summers. I've thought about being a jockey, but I don't know. I'll probably get too big." He grinned at me.

"Never!" I was being only half sarcastic. "How come you came back here?"

"Mom's softened up a little. Or maybe she was just sick of having me around. Anyhow, I'm on an extended visit. Dad enrolled me at MacGregor Academy for tenth grade."

"Then what?" I asked, keeping my voice casual.

"Back to Maryland."

I shut my mouth tightly against the chill wind that bustled between the buildings where we were leading our horses. I kept it shut even after we were inside the snug barn. I didn't want to ask any more questions because I might not like the answers.

I spent most of Christmas vacation with my dad in his efficiency apartment, with its white walls and balcony overlooking the parking lot. I felt weird and out of place. Nothing seemed right. The apartment even smelled funny, maybe because Dad was smoking again after two years without a cigarette. I found out he'd taken a job in Colorado.

"The sunny Southwest," he said. "That's where the good construction jobs are located. That's the place to be, and that's where I'm going."

"When?" I asked. The word tasted bitter.

"The end of February or early March. You'll be coming to visit me, Maria. You'll love it!" He reached across his dinette table and touched my cheek. "You'll finally get some tan on that pale face."

I jerked my head away. That night Dad took me out to eat and bought me strawberry shortcake for dessert. At first I wasn't going to eat it. Then I remembered what Colin had said about punishing himself instead of his parents. So I took a big spoonful and let the delightful flavor wipe out any desire to punish anyone.

Funny thing—that whole visit my father never once asked me about my horse.

In January the weather turned cold. Snow heaped against the buildings at Mason's Stables and was blown into tortured drifts in the lee of each fence.

Colin and I rode inside now. Usually there were other people riding, too, but I didn't mind, because I felt confident on Surprise. One day Sherri said, "Maria, you've really improved! Would you like to bring your horse to some of the shows with us this summer?"

All I could do was nod and grin. Colin gave me two thumbs up and smiled back at me.

Usually those first months of a year drag. That space between Christmas vacation and spring break seems to be an endless, frozen valley.

This year was different. The days flipped past like the pages of a calendar in one of those old movies. There were some I wanted to catch and press smooth to save forever. Like the day Colin was riding his dad's powerful Thoroughbred jumper, Make-a-Bet. They ripped around the arena, clearing hurdle after hurdle. With each jump my heart almost crashed.

"Good show!" yelled Sherri.

I couldn't say a word.

Later, while I was helping Colin cool Make-a-Bet down, I said, "I hope you never fall off."

"I already have. Lots of times. But not off Weasel." He patted the horse's sweaty neck.

"Weasel? How come you call him that?"

"'Cause he's quick and sly, and he goes 'pop' over jumps. You want to try him sometime?"

It took me a second to realize he wasn't joking, and my face grew warm with pleasure. "Sure," I answered. "Sometime."

Another day we had finished working our horses and had turned them out in the paddock when I got a phone call. It was my mother asking if I'd mind hanging around the stables because she had to work late.

"Perfect," said Colin when I told him. "I've got something to show you."

He brought Petunia, the placid, broad-backed mare, out of her stall, and I helped him groom her.

"You're going to ride *her?*" I asked incredulously.

"You think I don't know how?" Colin gave me one of his slow grins.

"Yeah . . . I mean no. I just don't get it."

"Just watch." Colin hopped onto Petunia bareback and trotted into the arena.

"Does his dad know what he's doing?" I heard a woman ask. I glanced around, but she was addressing someone else. Several other people had stopped grooming their horses and were leaning against the low wall, watching Colin and Petunia.

A circus routine. That's what he did. Standing on Petunia's back, the reins in one hand, Colin rode at a walk and then a slow canter. Next he sat down, sideways and backwards, while the mare trotted around the ring as if she'd been doing this all her life. Then he sprang off and sent her cantering off alone. Colin ran across the ring and leaped back on. I joined in the applause.

Colin did his final maneuver as the mare moved at a collected canter. He dropped the reins. A thin gasp came from somewhere behind me. As if that were his cue, Colin did a back flip. He landed on Petunia's rump and made a couple of quick steps to regain his balance. Then he eased into a sitting position and urged Petunia into a fast gallop. They pulled up in front of me, and Colin hopped off.

"I usually fall off doing that last bit," he admitted with a lopsided smile.

"You're crazy," I said.

"No. I'd be crazy if I tried that stuff without practicing. But I've been working out that routine for weeks."

I shook my head and rubbed Petunia behind her ears.

The first week in February I noticed a change in Colin. He was listening, and I was talking.

"Hey, what's the matter?" I demanded. "You haven't told me how to do anything for at least three days."

He didn't answer at first, busying himself with adjusting the stirrup leathers on Gem's saddle. The filly danced away, and he had to bring her back and make her stand still. It wasn't until he'd swung up into the saddle and gathered up his reins that he turned to me and said, "That's because you know everything now, Maria."

"Oh, yeah. Sure," I said sarcastically.

"Come on. Gem needs work on the left lead. Funny how most horses prefer one side or the other. Like being left- or right-handed."

That's better, I thought. Now he sounds like himself.

When Colin greeted me Friday afternoon, he was dressed in a down jacket, a wool cap, and leather gloves.

"What's with you? The side of the barn blow off or something?" I peered around him into the dusky interior of the building.

"We're going on a trail ride today."

"It's too cold," I protested. "My ears'll fall off! You

know, like Percival, your dad's cat that lost half his ears from frostbite."

"Maria, it's forty-five degrees. We're having a winter heat wave."

So we rode out across the fields and into the state park, where I'd never been before.

The two horses pranced through the deep, soft snow. Soon the dark-trunked trees cut us off from the sight of buildings, cars, and people.

"What do you think? You like this?" Colin asked.

"I love it!"

"Maria . . ." He hesitated.

"What?"

"Never mind. Let's race!"

"I've never even galloped," I said as my body tensed.

Colin and Gem took off in a splash of snow. I could barely hold Surprise back. So I let him go.

His first leap forward threw me into the saddle with a thump that almost dumped me into a drift. But I bounced forward and grabbed a handful of his mane and clung like lint. We galloped up a slope with the white froth spewing behind and around us. It was like a dream, racing on top of a cloud.

When we slowed to a walk, Colin dropped back to ride beside me.

"You look great," he said. There was a special sound in his voice that told me he wasn't referring to my riding form.

By the time we returned to the stables, my hands were hurting, and my nose felt like an icy knob on my face. We unsaddled and unbridled the horses, but it seemed to take forever for me to get done. My fingers were refusing to listen to my brain. Colin just stood there, waiting and watching me.

After turning both horses into the paddock, we saw them greet the other horses with nudges and little nips. I whistled, and Surprise looked at me with his small ears pricked.

As we put away our tack, I remarked, "My hands are still frozen."

Colin swung his saddle onto its rack and grabbed mine from me. He set it into place. Then he turned to me and without a word took my hands in his. We were still in the tack room, and the door had swung shut, but I felt awkward. What if someone walked in? And how could his hands be so warm? He moved closer, and I didn't move back.

"They're okay now," I whispered. "My hands."

"Maria," he said softly. His voice held a question. My answer was to tip my face up toward his and close my eyes. Then he kissed me. Once, and very gently.

"Maria," he said, "I have to leave. I've known for a week but just couldn't tell you." His voice sounded weird, rough and uncertain. I pulled my hands from his and looked down at the pebbly concrete floor with its scattering of hay and dirt.

"When?" I asked.

"Tomorrow morning. I'm flying back to Maryland. My mom's getting married and wants me there for the wedding and afterwards. Her new husband's got two kids, and they'll be living with us. Boys, one a year older than me and the other around ten. I have to be there, she says. So we can be a family."

"Oh." It felt as if that one little word were being torn out of me. My throat ached. "Are you . . . ever coming back?" I whispered. And will things be the same if you do? I wondered. I didn't ask.

"Sure. Maria?"

I looked at his face carefully. He seemed fragile suddenly, not like the confident boy on the fence or the one flipping on a horse's back. I liked him this way, too.

"I'm sorry," he whispered. "I meant to tell you every day. But it was so hard." He glanced away, as if this statement were difficult to face. "Anyhow," he added, his voice barely loud enough for me to hear, "I got you a going-away present."

"But *I'm* not going away," I said.

"Yeah . . . well . . . a Valentine's present, then." He reached into the pocket of his jacket and produced a tiny white box. He held it cupped in his hands.

Reaching out, I took it from him. I pried off the lid and plucked out the miniature square of cotton. I slipped my fingers under the dainty gold chain and held it up toward the one light bulb hanging from the center of the room. A heart-shaped pendant with an exquisite horse's head dangled from the center of the chain.

"I love it, Colin. Thanks."

It was time for me to leave. My mother would be arriving to pick me up in a few minutes. I hate good-byes. I guess Colin does, too. The last time I saw him, he was standing at the barn door, his hand raised in a half wave.

"See ya," he said, which was what he always said when I left for home.

I put on the necklace that night, and I haven't taken it off. Maybe I'll wear it forever.